I0692000

BEATING BANKS
AT THEIR OWN GAME

DON'T FEAR BIG BROTHER—FEAR BIG BANKS

STEVE LEVI
Master of the Impossible Crime

PUBLICATION
CONSULTANTS
We Believe In The Power Of Authors

PO Box 221974 Anchorage, Alaska 99522-1974
books@publicationconsultants.com—www.publicationconsultants.com

ISBN: 978-1-59433-822-9
eISBN: 978-1-59433-823-6
Library of Congress Catalog Card Number: 2018954274

CONTENTS

3

CHAPTER 1

THE ARREST OF HAROLD CHARLES DOBBINS

It would have been a fair bet that until the middle of March, the average person in Las Vegas had absolutely no idea what a codicil was. Most likely, they would never have even heard the term. If they had, they would have assumed it had something to do with entomology. A cocoon perhaps or the pupal stage of a cockroach or silverfish, the only bugs Las Vegans knew by sight.

And reputation.

It would also have been a safe bet to say that most Las Vegans knew beans about bugs and only thought of them in the collective—like when they called Terminix to complain that they were being overrun by vermin and had no idea what to do. Older Las Vegans had heard of Melvin Earle Dummar, of course—everyone in the casino industry had. But that name was from an era both long gone and forgotten.

Neither of these tidbits made a whit of difference to the three Internal Revenue Service (IRS) agents who banged rudely on Harold Charles Dobbin's door that Sunday morning at an hour when only the righteous were up and getting dressed for church. Dobbins was not a churchgoer, so he was still in bed. He had intended to stay in bed for at least another three hours. It was not that he was nursing a case of the Bourbon flu or was with someone he had met the night before in a low-light nightclub. It was just that he slept in late since his forced retirement from the Cypress Casino five years ago.

Life had been going reasonably well for him for a good four decades and then, one day, he was out on the street, squeezed out by a cadre of young bucks. They had gone to night school together and looked upon at anyone older than 30 as a dinosaur. Dobbins was a few years beyond 70, so he wasn't just a dinosaur; he was the progenitor thereof.

No casino wanted an old codger in their accounting room, so he was forced to get a job with his stepfather's younger sister at the title company where she worked. The casino job had been humdrum with numbers; the title company was humdrum with signatures. Both jobs required meticulous attention to detail. Both jobs were mentally b-o-r-i-n-g and that was the reason Dobbins slept in on the mornings when he did not have to be at work at the crack of dawn, which, in Las Vegas, was 9 o'clock.

Dobbins was living well below his previous means but had come to accept the fact that he was now permanently downsized. The only saving grace was that he was old enough to collect his pension and Social Security at the same time he was able to work full time. But it was a very small blessing. Then, again, he didn't need much subsistence money. He could walk to the grocery store and get an alcoholic high from a can of beer, so, at 72, widowed with no children in Las Vegas, he was doing just fine.

But he knew he was running in place.

One medical procedure and he was going to be in a financial bind. Other than that fear, his life was sedate, measured, and predictable. He was in a rut and reluctantly beginning to be happy to finish his grand adventure that way. His somber, elderly happiness changed at 7:01 a.m. on one particular day—March 15.

The interruption into his life of enforced tranquility came in the form of IRS agents—three of them, identical in stature and attitude, mousey and rude, and only slightly different in dress. They banged on his screen—ignoring the doorbell—until he opened the pine slab of his front door and stared at the three middle-aged women in the pitiless glare of a Las Vegas Sunday sun. They asked whether he was Harold Charles Dobbins and whether he was related to Jean Peters. He said he was Harold Charles Dobbins but no, he was not related to Jean Peters; he only worked at her title company.

Then they asked if he was related to Dolores Dobbins, Geraldine Jones, and Myrrh Frankincense. He replied in the affirmative. "Sort of," he said. Dolores was his spinster aunt, his stepfather's unmarried younger sister, and she worked in the same title company where he worked, the Peters Title Company. Myrrh Frankincense was her lesbian partner and not a blood relative. Myrrh had been a foundling whom no one had wanted. At 18, when she was no longer eligible for orphanage patronage, she had joined the army. The name on her orphanage paperwork had listed her as Geraldine Jones, two names clearly pulled out of a hat, so she changed her two names on her enlistment papers to Myrrh Frankincense. She found herself doubly precious even though no one else did. The name change raised a stink with the army and the Selective Service, which took a decade to resolve. She eventually became, officially, Myrrh Frankincense, and the Geraldine Jones part of her life slipped into the dark recesses of Las Vegas historical records.

Until this morning.

Dobbins stated that he was not a nephew of Myrrh Frankincense but knew she had once been Geraldine Jones. But she was aunt in name only. Dolores and Myrrh had met when the two were young, in the 1960s, and had both been card dealers in one of the casinos long gone and had spent considerable time together. In fact, they had spent so much time together that it was rumored they were lesbians. This rumor was true, and the two women spent years as a couple in the one city in the United States where no one cared if you were lesbian, Caspian, or thespian as long as you had money for tips and shows. Both women were still alive because he worked with them at the title company and had seen them—alive—18 hours earlier. He ogled the three badges and asked why the IRS wanted to know the obvious.

Nothing he said seemed to make any difference to the agents. They asked to come into his home. Dobbins replied that he did not have four chairs, as he did not need such. The agents insisted and came in anyway. Dobbins indicated one of two chairs in a part of his home charitably called a dining room. One of the agents, the oldest one, snapped an identification flip-wallet from out of a holster on her belt as if it were a pistol. She was Jane Titterington, and her name was followed by some bold letters followed by periods. He didn't see any listing of her title, just "Internal Revenue Service" in big letters beneath her name. Had her name been shorter, the "Internal Revenue Service" lettering would have been larger than her name.

As Titterington sat, Dobbins pushed the salt-and-pepper napkin-holder centerpiece aside. He took the other chair and put his elbows down on the unsteady table. Titterington professionally flipped open a folder and laid it flat on the table. (Did she practice that?) She slowly turned over sheets of paper as if she were looking for one particular document.

Dobbins knew her actions were for show. Someone who had never had to deal with the IRS would have been intimidated. But Dobbins had been through four decades of audits by the IRS, Security and Exchange Commission (SEC), State of Nevada Gaming Control Board, State of Nevada Department of Banking, Cypress Casino in-house auditor, and several court-ordered audits, so this was not his first fiscal rodeo. For Dobbins, Titterington's theatrics were a wasted effort.

Finally, Titterington stopped looking through the pile of papers and pulled a sheet off the top with her right thumb and forefinger with an expression of "Ah-ha! Here you are."

Dobbins was unimpressed.

Then Titterington looked up at Dobbins and asked when was the last he had seen Jean Peters. The other two agents stood like large beetles on either side of the front door.

"Thursday afternoon. Why?" he replied.

"How about Myrrh Frankincense?"

"Friday afternoon."

"Do you know where Jean Peters is now?"

Dobbins looked at Titterington oddly. Then he looked over his shoulder at the agents at the door. His gaze returned to Titterington, and he said, "I just answered that question. We all work together. Why are you here?"

"Ever hear of Melvin Earle Dummar?"

"Yeah. Long time ago. Said Howard Hughes owed him big bucks from a will on a paper bag. Something like that. Turned out to be a phony. Right?"

"Ever hear of Howard Hughes?"

This was a stupid question to a man who had lived in Las Vegas for more than half a century and worked in a casino for 53 of those years.

"I just said I did. Sure. He's a legend here in Vegas. Come on, you people know that! You can't live in Vegas and not know who Howard Hughes was! But he died a long time ago. Back in the 1970s. Why?"

Titterington ignored the question. "How about Jean Peters?"

"Yeah, I know her. I just told you I work for her. She owns the Peters Title Company where I work," he said, tired of the verbal dueling. "Now I've been very polite and answered your inquiries. It's early on Sunday morning, and I am through answering stupid questions. Either tell me why you're here or leave."

All three agents glanced around at each other, sending secret IRS glance messages. One of the women at the door nodded to Titterington. Titterington rose without saying a word. All three agents turned, in unison, and left.

"Hey!" shouted Dobbins. "What's going on?"

Dobbins followed the IRS agents through his front door and out onto what in Las Vegas is called a lawn, but the rest of America calls burnt grass spotted with healthy dandelions. He didn't get an answer from the IRS agents because they, on their way out, were replaced by a pair of Las Vegas policemen on their way in.

"You Harold Charles Dobbins?"

9

"Yeah. Who are you?"

"Police," one of the men said as he pointed to his badge, "Las Vegas police."

"I'm so happy you told me that," snapped Dobbins. "I could *not* have figured that out on my own."

"Well, while you are figuring that out *on your own*," growled the older of the two, a 20-something officer with the attitude of a derivatives trader, "what is your relationship to Jean Peters, Dolores Dobbins, and Myrrh Frankincense?"

"This is getting tiresome. Why don't you ask those people?" Dobbins pointed to the retreating IRS agents. "I just answered that question for them."

"Why don't you just answer *our* question?" The Las Vegas police stood solid in their dress blues like juniper trees, in Dobbins's front yard, fixtures unknown in Las Vegas—the juniper trees, not policemen.

"Jean Peters owns the title company where I work. Dolores Dobbins is my aunt. I work with her and Myrrh Frankincense at the title company. Why are you here?"

"*We* ask the questions around here!" snapped the younger of the officers.

"Not on my property, you don't!" said a riled Dobbins. "Do you have a warrant?"

"As a matter of fact," the old officer stated officially, "we do." He pulled a folded paper out of his shirt pocket and handed it to Dobbins. "Do you have any pets in the home? Is the stove on inside?"

"No. Why?" asked Dobbins as he started to unfold the paper.

"Because," said the younger cop producing handcuffs, "you are going to be downtown for a while."

The younger cop step forward, grabbed Dobbins's left wrist, and twisted it behind him. As Dobbins juggled the folded paper and protested that he had not yet read the warrant, the older cop said, "That's called *resisting arrest.* You are really racking up the charges today." Then the second wrist was clipped to the first. Dobbins still had the warrant in his right hand, and it was flopping back and forth as his wrist were chained together. It was going to be a while before he was going to be able to read it.

Then, in full view of his neighbors on their way to church and the three IRS agents who were standing hip-to-briefcase-to-hip on the sidewalk side of the drab picket fence, Dobbins's five-foot-three frame was duck-walked out to the gutter lip and jammed into the back of a Las Vegas police car. With goo-goo eyes, his neighbors watched as he was whisked away, sirens blaring and bubblegum lights flashing. If there had been someone left to lock up his home, Dobbins didn't see them.

Having spent six years in the Navy, Dobbins would have called his escort to the Las Vegas Police Department a short convoy. He would not have called it a convoy at all until the older Las Vegas policeman got on the radio and said that the individual involved in the "Hughes matter" was on his way to the station. Within moments the Las Vegas police vehicle and the unmarked IRS agents' car acquired a tail of vans with television-station logos on their side. Then it was a convoy. At the downtown station, there was a gaggle of photographers overflowing the sidewalk and standing in the gutter snapping shots of Dobbins as he zipped by in the patrol car on his way into the underground garage.

Once inside the parking garage, Dobbins was hustled—carried more than allowed to walk—down a corridor and thrust into some place that looked like a medical room. The warrant was pulled from his hand, and he was uncuffed. He was immediately stripped of his bathrobe and pajamas and given a pair of brittle underpants and greasy-looking T-shirt with holes under the armpits. He put the underpants and T-shirt on quickly, embarrassed to be naked in front of a dozen people he did not know. When he stood up, he was ordered into a jumpsuit. This jumpsuit was not the usual florescent orange seen-along-the-highway-as-the-convicts-pick-up-trash with the LVPD on the back. It was gray, with the letters MWLVPD stenciled on the front. His bedroom slippers were dropped into an evidence bag, and he was given a pair of sandals the thickness of tissue paper. Then he was handcuffed again, this time with his wrists in the front.

11

Protesting the whole time, he was again dragged more than walked down an antiseptic-smelling corridor and dumped more than escorted into an interrogation room. He recognized the interrogation room from the hundreds of cops-and-robbers movies and television dramas he had watched, many of them over the past five years while he was retired, semiretired, marginally employed, or too tired to sleep. The chain between the two handcuffs was clamped inside a metal hoop in the center of a table. He was contemplating what was going to happen next when a young woman in a LVPD uniform, the age of his daughter—if he had had a daughter—came in and offered him a form in triplicate.

"What's this?"

"Your Miranda warning."

"My what?"

"Miranda warning. Do you know what your Miranda rights are?"

"You mean the right to remain silent and all those other things the cops say on TV shows?"

"Yes. If you sign this, it means you understand your rights and everything you say . . ."

"I know that part. What happens if I don't sign?"

"You go right to jail until you go before a judge for your arraignment tomorrow."

"What's the charge? I mean, what did I do?"

"There is no charge," she paused for a long moment, "yet." She again gave a long pause and then said, "Right now you're just being held as a material witness." She pointed to his chest. "That's what the MWLVPD on your jumpsuit stands for."

Dobbins looked down at the upside-down MWLVP on his jumpsuit vest. "But I haven't done anything wrong."

"Then sign the Miranda warning, and tell it to the detectives."

Dobbins signed.

The young woman tore off the back copy of the Miranda form and thrust it toward him. Then she handed him the warrant he had not yet been able to read in his front yard or in the back seat of the squad car. Without a word she vaporized, like a rabbit into a magician's hat.

The warrant told him nothing. In fact, it wasn't a warrant at all—at least the way he understood what a warrant was.

He wasn't actually under arrest. He was being detained as a material witness in a suspected fraudulent codicil in the alleged possession of one Jean Peters who had filed a probate will leaving all her property to Harold Charles Dobbins of Las Vegas. Inked in at the bottom of the page was a handwritten note that Dobbins had "resisted arrest" and was signed with a name so badly scrawled that he could not read it.

Without warning, the door to the interrogation room burst inward, and a dozen—a full dozen—men and women flooded in. There was only one other chair in the room and that was taken by Titterington, the same IRS agent who had questioned Dobbins in his home.

"Comfy?" asked the Titterington.

"What do you think," snapped Dobbins as he rattled his handcuffs. "Why am I here?"

"You don't know?" said Titterington in fake surprise.

"I read this warrant," said Dobbins, kind of tossing the paperwork across the table as best as he could being in handcuffs that were secured to the center of the table. "It's not actually a warrant the way I understand warrants. It tells me nothing. What's a codicil?"

"Codicil," said Titterington superciliously, "is a testamentary document. Like a will. Usually it's part of a will. In this case, a part of a will, an amendment."

"Which has what to do with me?"

"It has everything to do with you. For starters, we'd like the fifty million dollars back."

Dobbins gave a surprised look. "You want *what* fifty million dollars back?"

"The fifty million dollars Jean Peters got from Howard Hughes that you have hidden."

Dobbins laughed. "You are kidding, right? I never got fifty million dollars from Howard Hughes. I never met Howard Hughes. I don't even know anyone who knew Howard Hughes. He died, what, fifty years ago? I don't know what you are talking about!"

"You don't know what I'm talking about?"

Dobbins looked at Titterington with disdain. "Are we going to play the same game here we did at my home—I answer a question, and you ask the same question again? You're like my late wife. Could never hear the answer I gave. Had to ask the same question six, seven times."

"So you are not going to tell us where you hid the fifty million dollars?"

"I haven't made fifty million dollars in my life. If I had fifty million dollars, I'd be living in Maui."

"I see," Titterington said and took a long pause in obvious stall for time. "We don't believe you."

"Then I've got a better question for you," snapped Dobbins as he leaned forward in anger. "What makes you think I have fifty million dollars?"

"Because we can't find it." Titterington smiled evilly. "We got a tip that you have been holding the fifty million dollars for Jean Peters, slowly slipping it into accounts unknown at this time. When she dies, you get all the money."

"Jean Peters never had that kind of money. My family never had that kind of money. We all came from farming stock. We didn't have squat. We don't have squat."

"But Jean Peters had fifty million dollars, and now it's gone."

"I was an accountant for fifty-three years," snapped Dobbins. "You can't hide that kind of money. How do you even know Jean Peters ever had fifty million dollars to give to anyone? She never told me she had that kind of money, and I've known her for years."

"We have our sources."

"You're saying that Howard Hughes gave Jean Peters the fifty million dollars in the first place? Why would he do that?"

"You tell me."

"I haven't a clue."

"Well, here's what we think." Titterington kind of rotated her head and gave it a dip to indicate the gathered throng. "A Jean Peters was Howard Hughes's first wife. We think he confused his Jean Peters with your Jean Peters, and your Jean Peters ended up with the fifty million dollars."

14

Dobbins was silent for a moment. Then he said, "Let me get this straight. Jean Peters was Howard Hughes first wife. He divorces here in, what, the 1960s."

"1971."

"OK, 1971. Hughes dies about 1976, five years later."

"That's right. He died in 1976."

"So you are telling me that Howard Hughes mixed up his first wife with the Jean Peters I know and gave the Jean Peters I know fifty million dollars, and none of his accountants knew about it, and none of his heirs knew about it, and now, fifty years later, it suddenly pops up? Let me the see the document."

"We don't have the document. We know it exists. We know Jean Peters has it. We're waiting to get her safety-deposit box drilled. That's where we believe the original document is located."

"*What!* You are holding me as a material witness based on a document you have not seen, do not know is authentic, and have yet to see it? What kind of a Mickey Mouse operation are you running?"

Titterington didn't break her cool. "We have documentary evidence that Jean Peters, the Jean Peters you know, the Jean Peters of Peters Title Company, received fifty million dollars. She does not have the money now. You are the heir to her estate. You are a man who knows how to hide the money until it is time for it to be revealed. Ergo, you know where the money is."

"I don't know anything about any money left to the Jean Peters I know. But as an accountant, again, I can tell you that it's almost impossible to hide fifty million dollars—particularly in this town. Not only does the Nevada Gaming Control Board overlook the books of every casino in the state, so does the FBI, the SEC, and the IRS. Then there are State of Nevada banking auditor. Every partner in every casino in Las Vegas has their own cadre of accountants. I know. I've been in this business since the 1970s. You can't hide that kind of money."

He paused for a moment. "I also find it very hard to believe that you could hide that kind of money from Howard Hughes's accountants. That kind of money may have been pin money to Hughes personally, but he had the best bean counters in the business. If there were fifty million dollars missing, they would have found it. They would have found it l-o-n-g ago. What am I missing here?"

Then—now that Dobbins was recovering from the shock of the faux arrest—it occurred to him that there was a very large legal chasm that the IRS was trying to leap in a single bound. Dobbins went in for the kill. "Even if it were true that I had this alleged fifty million dollars, any statute of limitation has since long run out. Even if fraud were involved, the statute of limitations would have run out on that as well. So what the hell are we really talking about here?"

There was a moment of silence.

Finally, one of the IRS agents spoke from the crowd behind Dobbins. "Fruit from a poisoned tree. There is no solid statute of limitations on fraud. Besides, Jean Peters's will has yet to be probated. So, technically, what you inherit will be stolen property. That restarts the clock on the statute of limitations."

"That's a crock," snapped Dobbins. "Any first-year law student knows that. Even if I had the fifty million dollars—which I do not—you'd have to prove fraud all the way back to 1971 and then prove I knew of the fraud in 1971. I was still in the navy then. I hadn't even started college."

None of this fazed the minions of the Department of the Treasury in the least. "We think you are lying," Titterington said in a flat voice. "That is a federal offense as well. That starts a new clock."

Dobbins was now feeling his oats. "I don't care what you *think*. I care what you can *prove*. You can't prove I have fifty million dollars, because I don't have that kind of money. I have never had that kind of money. I don't believe you can launder that kind of money in this town and not be spotted by any one of a dozen state and federal agencies, not to mention gads of accounting firms hired to look for loose money just like this fifty million dollars you say I have. I doubt Howard Hughes could have hidden that kind of money even with his millions. I find it hard to believe that the Jean Peters I know ever had that kind of money at any time in her life. Where's your proof?"

"Well, we have our sources." It was a deep voice from the back of the crowd.

Now Dobbins was angry. "Let's see if I have this right. You have an *anonymous* source who says I got fifty million dollars from a codicil—codicil, is that right? —a codicil written by Howard Hughes, a man who has been dead fifty years, whom I never met, who died in a state I have never visited, and this is the *basis* of my arrest?"

"You are not under arrest," cut in someone else from the crowd. "You are a material witness. That's what the MWLVPD means. You are not under arrest. We are holding you pending release and authentication of the codicil that we have been reliably informed is a forgery."

"You don't even have the codicil that says I got fifty million dollars?! You're arresting me on a rumor?"

"You are not under arrest, and it is not a rumor. It is from a source we consider reliable. We will be holding you for a day or two as a material witness until we can clear up this matter."

"You can't do that. I have rights! What about all those television crews and newspaper people? Where did they come from? Never-Never Land? Did you tell them about this matter?"

"No, we did not. But this is a free country, Mr. Dobbins, and what the press does is the press' business, not ours."

"Call a lawyer, you'll be here for a while." It was a woman's voice from the body of the assembled.

"I can't afford a lawyer!"

"Use some of the fifty million dollars you say you don't have," snapped someone else in the back of the crowd. "We're going to find it anyway."

CHAPTER 2

SANDOVAL "BULLET" WISNOSKI

Sandoval John Wisnoski could have been a body-double stand-in for Benito Mussolini—and Wisnoski wasn't even Italian. He had the same squat frame and natural baldpate that made his head look like the nose of a bullet slug; thus his nickname: Bullet. His official title at the Triple Pines Casino was Vice-President of Casino Operations, which did not at all describe—or hint—at what he really did. It described what he did *not do*. Rather, as in most businesses, the title "vice-president" is reserved for those who do absolutely nothing because he or she is the son or daughter of the president of the corporation or is assigned those actions that are too unsavory for the president or board of directors to know about. A combination of hatchet man and gravedigger, Bullet resolved unsolvable problems that, from time to time, cropped up at Triple Pines. He was a shade under 70 and had been with the casino longer than some of the other employees had been alive.

For anyone under the age of 40, there is no occupational definition for the function Bullet performed. This is because America was sucked into the black hole of PC—political correctness—in the late 1990s. Suddenly American English decomposed into a cesspool of linguistic

18

confusion. Before 1998, a "dumb f#%&" had a specific meaning. It was someone who was so stupid that he or she did not understand the mistake he or she had made even after it had been explained to him or her. But this was not the end of the definition. A "dumb f#%&" was so stupid when a similar circumstance occurred again that he or she would make the same mistake again. "Dumb f#%&" on the West Coast was shortened to "DF," and when it was used, everyone knew what the acronym meant. By 2005, the definition of "DF" was softened to "dumb folk," which not only lacked the specificity of "dumb f#%&" but also implied that there were a host of people just like the individual who was a "DF." This is not accurate. True DFs are untrainable. Everyone makes mistakes, some of them whoppers. Most of us learn from those mistakes even if we make them two or three times. But a DF before 1998 was a specific idiot who would not, could not, and did not learn the basics. The term itself was precise in its meaning, and all someone—in 1995—had to do was say that Harry in Personnel was a DF, and the new boss would know exactly what was meant. Other popular acronyms of that era included FI (f#%&ing idiot) for someone who made a dangerous, stupid mistake after being instructed not to do so; SOL (s&*% out of luck) for being forced to live with a terrible situation that was beyond one's control and could not be adjusted; and FUBAR (f#%&ed up beyond all repair), a piece of equipment or social circumstance that was so unbelievably, well, f#%&ed up so badly that it could not be repaired. Every generation had its acronyms. The preceding generations used acronyms such as SOS (s&*% on a shingle) for U.S. military-issue creamed, chipped beef on a cracker served to troops during the Second World War; NAVY (never again volunteer yourself); and SNAFU (Situation Normal; All F&*%ed Up.).

After 2000, and particularly after the election of America's first black president, any terms that hinted of a sexual activity or racial minority or had a scatological root were banned. "Blacks," "negroes," and "coloreds" became "African Americans," and one had to be careful not to use the words "spade," "niggardly" or "raccoon" even though all three had specific, nonracial definitions. "Red Skins" became "Indians" and the intolerable, never changing office routine previously known as the "Rat Race" became the "Same Old/Same Old." "F&*%ed up" became "fouled up" and "doesn't give a s&*%" became "doesn't give a rat's ass" or "doesn't give a hairy rat's ass." And, in print, the offending letters—offending *letters?* —were replaced with symbols.

Had one been born before about 1960, he—the PC equivalent of him or her a generation later—would have known exactly what a hatchet man was. A hatchet man is the person who did the dirty work that the boss should not do, could not do, would not do or wanted someone else to take the blame for doing. The world is a very dirty place, whether you are in business, politics, or social climbing. Someone must be the face of the hostile takeover, the throwing of a candidate under the electoral bus, or spreading the truth/rumor that one of the prom-queen candidates is pregnant. A real-world example of an efficient hatchet man is the CIA. When something very nasty has to be done outside the United States, the CIA does it. If it goes right, the president of the United States will claim that his policies were instrumental in making "that possible." If the situation gets out of hand, the president can always blame an "out of control CIA" and demand "internal changes."

Historically, the best hatchet man in American history was Andrew Jackson. He was General Andrew Jackson before he became President of the United States. In 1817, after Jackson's stunning defeat of the British in the Battle of New Orleans, President James Monroe ordered Jackson to lead an expedition against the Seminole Indians in what was then Georgia. Monroe was no political slouch. The Seminole War had "bad idea" written all over it. But he really didn't have any choice but to intervene. Politics, you know.

So he did what all wily politicians do: he put some "reasonable deniability" between himself and the problems he knew were coming down the pike. Things were going to get very dicey very quickly, and it was very likely—rather most likely—that Jackson would *meander* into Spanish territory. That Spanish territory is now called Florida. Americans wanted Florida, but the president of the United States could hardly order General Andrew Jackson to invade a foreign country and seize it.

After all, a Declaration of War was a specific right of Congress.

So President Monroe did what is today called an "end around run."

He didn't *tell* Jackson to invade Florida. But then, again, he *did not tell General Jackson not to invade* Florida either. He knew that the United States was going to war against the Seminole Indians in an area where the border between the United States and Spanish Florida was imprecise. Thus, Jackson *would necessarily* have to be tiptoeing along a nebulous, unmarked border in the swamps and wilderness that separated the United States from Spanish Florida. To cover his presidential and, therefore, political posterior, Monroe gave vague instructions. Jackson's orders were to "terminate the conflict" with the Seminole Indians.

Andrew Jackson was not a fool.

He was also an expansionist.

He knew exactly what the President wanted.

He had no problem taking Florida for the United States.

But he was also a wily politician. He knew how to cover his own posterior. As he was militarily tiptoeing along the Florida border, he—allegedly—sent a missive to President Monroe, which stated, "Let it be signified to me through any channel that the possession of the Floridas would be desirable to the United States, and in sixty days it will be accomplished." Being politically correct for this age—but only after the fecal matter struck the rotating metal blade—President Monroe claimed he *had never received* the missive from Jackson.

It didn't matter.

Jackson had already taken Florida.

The Spanish protested to no avail. Eventually Secretary of State John Quincy Adams negotiated the sale of Florida to the United States and promised the Spanish that something *would be done* to punish that horrible man (Andrew Jackson) for his unauthorized invasion of Florida. Something was done to punish Jackson: he became the first territorial governor of the Florida territory. History does not record how the Spanish felt about this *punishment.*

Like Andrew Jackson, Bullet was a hatchet man. He, like Jackson, was also very good at his job. Proof was his tenure at the Triple Pines.

Hatchet men have a tendency to move around a lot. They are hired to clean up messes. Once the mess is cleaned up, they move on because of the animosity they have engendered doing their job. That way when employees complain about how badly they were being treated, the boss can say "Well, that was so-and-so and he's gone now. Let's start fresh!"

Hatchet men usually generate a tsunami of suspicion and bad feeling, particularly if they come from outside the workplace. Whatever they do, it leads to employee unrest. Even if the hatchet men are removing office idiots, the hatchet men are still looked upon as pariahs. After all, the general feeling is that the office blatherskite may be a blithering idiot, but he's *our* idiot, and there is a certain amount of propriety.

No office has a good day when the hatchet men are on the prowl. No matter how well you are doing your job, everyone assumes their job is on the line. A lot of firing, "downsizing," and "moving on" is political, and most employees look up the administrative food chain and wonder which change in the direction of the political wind is going to blow them overboard.

Bullet, however, was very different. He was very good at his job. He had longevity at the Triple Pines because he did not play politics and was honest in the sense that he did have favorites. If you did your job well even if he personally disliked you, your position was safe. Even better, he kept upper management from meddling in the trenches below. He was a buffer who kept the casino management bulls&*% confined to the sixth floor, not on the mezzanine or in the counting rooms. The experienced card dealers and pit bosses knew exactly how important that was. They had to live and die by not only the state and federal rules, statute, and regulations but also the inane whims of management. At the very least, Bullet was on their side. If you got the boot from Bullet, you deserved it.

Bullet was also respected at the administrative level. He was the hard nose when such a proboscis was needed. In the world of casinos, such is always needed. With so much oversight by so many state and federal agencies, one slip could be disastrous. Additionally, the casinos had to contend with public relations more than any other industry in America. The Las Vegas Strip had a carefully crafted, constantly fine-tuned reputation across the country, and all it would take was one bad incident to ruin tens of millions of dollars of good will generated by television advertising, magazine stories, and catering the eccentric whims of movie and television producers who wanted to film in Las Vegas. From the A-list celebrities and executive producers to the fly-by-night production company staff who wanted a Las Vegas setting simply as an excuse to get a free trip to the Strip, every casino, restaurant, hotel, and theme-park person had to smile and say, "What else can I do for you?" no matter how ridiculous the request.

A good example of the kind of executive-level problem that Bullet was adapt at resolving was the case of the Triple Pines Head of Security. This man only reported to the Triple Pines president and that man had the spine of a jellyfish. As long as whatever was happening was not illegal or slowed the gaming tables, the president could have given a hairy rat's ass. The problem was that every negative twitch in any casino for any reason would create a hairy rat's ass of a problem—particularly if the newspapers reported it. Reporters were always looking for a good story, and sometimes when there was not a good story available, the press would find a molehill and pile it into a mountain.

The problem with the Triple Pines head of security was that he had a growing drug problem acerbated by a pending divorce. He was also spiraling toward the bottom of an alcoholic whirlpool, stumbling through a souring affair with a B-girl and had a DUI that had been "made to go away" by the casino. This man was headed for a major meltdown.

But—and it was a very big *but*—his parents were major shareholders in the Triple Pines, and they were on the A-list of the social movers and shakers in Las Vegas. Whatever it was that Bullet did, it worked. The head of security went straight and sober. The rest of his life fell apart, but he was able to face his problems and pull his life back together without a line of coke on his coffee table or a shot glass of Scotch in his hand.

After four decades at the Triple Pines, no one ever asked what Bullet was doing. No one wanted to know. No one dared to know. He was like a 300-pound bomb in the trail. Everyone knew it was there and they gingerly avoided it. All anyone needed to know was that whether they were in Bullet's cross hairs, and, after four decades at the Triple Pines, everyone knew that as long as they did their job, Bullet would not be looking at them. But everyone also knew that when there was dirty work to be done, Bullet was the one who did it.

Bullet had come into his present occupation through a rather odd side door. He began his occupational life as a purple squirrel, someone who had sterling credentials in a field in which he had no academic degree. In his case, it was medicine. As a young man, he had absolutely no interest in the mind-numbing rote of the high school curriculum, so he dropped out. He played hide-and-seek with the truant officers until he turned 17 and lied about his age and enlisted in the U.S. army. That was in 1963, and he had signed up for a six-year hitch. He had an IQ of 162, which meant nothing to him but did mean quite a bit to the tarnished brass who were then establishing field priorities for a brush fire war in a place called Vietnam. This recruit had brains and the ability to learn. So he was trained as a medic. This was no big deal in 1963 because when one was a medic in the army in 1963, you were basically a glorified orderly in a hospital and assigned to some godforsaken military hospital located at the outskirts of some godforsaken town in a state where hot water had yet to be discovered.

That was in 1963.

By the time he finished Basic, it was 1964.

Under President Lyndon Johnson, those godforsaken military hospitals were suddenly MASH units, and everyone in medicine with a uniform served in the surgical tents—that is, the doctors served under the canvas. Bullet served under a canopy of green. He arrived in Vietnam when the United States was still battling the Viet Cong for the hearts and minds of the Vietnamese people. To Bullet, this just meant he was spending more time servicing Central Highland villagers than military personnel. He would be escorted into a village by combined American and South Vietnamese units where he would bring the wonders of modern medicine to people who had to live in huts made of bamboo and drank water from abandoned ammunition cans. Along with becoming an expert in difficult childbirths, treating dysentery, and inoculating children against smallpox, he picked up conversational French and enough Vietnamese to understand the ills of his patients without an interpreter. The touchy-feely era ended with the arrival of the Tet. Within a matter of weeks, he was handling napalm burns, performing what would be called surgery in America on the earth humps between rice paddies, scooping intestines back into disemboweled marines and being a mobile pharmaceutical dispensary. After extending twice because he was in a critical field, he came back stateside when the fraud of Vietnamization descended into civil war. Months after it became clear that the United States could not win in Southeast Asia, Bullet and what was left of the American command in the field was pulled out of the festering wound of the Mekong Delta.

He came home with jungle rot in his crotch, but he did not have a monkey on his back. If there was any one thing that was universal among the hale and hardy in the jungle, bars, alleys, brothels, and barracks in the war zone, it was the willingness to experiment with drugs. It was actually more than a willingness; it was a proof of fraternity. It was not called "using" but "getting on." There was nothing "bad" about the drugs. They were there to be used. Like the bar girls. Both were made to be used. Someday you would regret them, of course, but at 18, 19, and 20, what was the harm in blowing steam?

The harm, Bullet the medic knew, was that there was no such a thing as a "little bit" of drugs. Those who said they were being recreational were fooling themselves. There are no recreational drugs. Like pornography, extended usage requires greater strength and variety. Yes, he had seen many boys smoke dope and nothing more. But those boys grew up quickly and realized they were on the wrong road of life. Those who felt they could "quit any time they wanted" were fools. At 18, 19, and 20, when you were tromping into and out of a jungle for ten days at a time, you could sweat out the demons. But back on the chaise lounge in Detroit, you didn't use drugs—the drugs used you. Of the dozen close GI buddies who came home with Bullet, half died of drugs before their thirties and, of the other half, only two remained alive, badly scarred from war, drugs, and the holocaust the drugs brought to their second, third, and fourth marriages and families.

Arriving stateside, Bullet was just another unemployed veteran. In spite of the fact that he had eight years of on-the-ground real-world experience with traumatic medical emergencies, he did not have a high school diploma and had not bothered to take the GED. So he could not get an EMT certificate. Therefore, he did not have a Chinaman's chance of working in the industry in which he was the most qualified in the community. He was just another purple squirrel.

What he did have was an uncle in Los Vegas, who could get him a job as a dealer.

So off to Las Vegas he went, from the jungles of Southeast Asia to the jingles of Las Vegas.

CHAPTER 3

LAS VEGAS SCANDAL, INC.

Frankly, when he received the photocopy of the Hughes Codicil that had been left in a Manilla envelope outside his office door, Walter Otterburg, publisher/editor/reporter for *Las Vegas Scandal, Inc.* did not know what to do about it.

If anything.

On one hand, he was sure it was a fake. After all, the old fart had been dead since 1976, and his first wife, Jean Peters, had not been around since 2000. He knew who Howard Hughes was even though the man had been dead longer than Otterburg had been alive. Jean Peters was a blank, so he had to Google her. Only then did he know she had been an actress in her own right and had abandoned the profession after she had married Hughes. When he looked at her stock shots on Wikipedia, she did look vaguely familiar. The list of movies in which she stared was not even that. He was sure he had seen the titles listed on some of the late-late-late night cable channels or Turner Classic Movies, but not one of the names of any one of the films rang even a distant bell. So, at best, this alleged copy of an alleged codicil was, at the very best even if authentic, a historical document. Nothing more.

27

But it was dated in 1971, and at that time—according to Wikipedia—Hughes and Peters were in the process of getting divorced. The signature looked authentic. Then, again, on a photocopy, any signature can *look* authentic. Even Melvin Earl Dummar had what appeared to be Hughes's signature on a will, but it had turned out to be as phony as a Las Vegas promise.

Again, then again, stranger things in the world had happened, so the sudden appearance of an historical document no one had previously known existed was possible. This was, after all, Las Vegas, and in Las Vegas "your dreams could come true."

Except if you worked here.

Then there was this $50 million.

That was quite a kicker.

Without the reference to the $50 million, the Hughes Codicil was just another imaginary log on the campfire of some Howard Hughes conspiracy garbanzo bean nut. But with the $50 million, there could be footprints to follow. Money does not just appear—or disappear—into thin air. As long as it is in the United States, its trail can be followed. Once it flies off to the Cayman Islands or the Bahamas, that's a different story. But this $50 million was supposedly received here in Las Vegas. That meant it was probably spent or invested here.

Maybe.

But it could be followed.

If the codicil is authentic.

Even if it was not authentic, it was still a juicy story.

That's because there's always a need for a story in the 24-hour-a-day news cycle. After all, a baby pulled from a cistern can make headlines for two weeks.

But Otterburg had to be journalistically careful.

He was sure the document was a fake. Publishing a story about a fake document was no story at all. It was just supermarket tabloidal. Yes, it was an interesting story. Yes, it had the trappings of a sensational storyline. But the codicil was clearly a fake. It had to be a fake. So where was the story?

The story, Otterburg reasoned, was going to be in how he handled the document. Cleverly done, he could stretch the story out for a few issues. *Issues* were the operational word here. *Issues* meant advertising in the plural. *Issues* meant follow-up stores in the multiples and newsstand sales in the scores. So what was a little white lie among people who knew better? Or, if they did not know better, it could hurt no one because everyone associated with the alleged-to-be-authentic-but-really-fake-and-everyone-with-the-brains-of-a-codfish-knew-it codicil was dead. Carefully handled, he could make a dime or two off this story.

He decided to run with it.

The drunk had told Otterburg that he was the only newsperson with a copy of the codicil. She could have been lying. Drunks have been known to do that. But whether she was lying or not, at this moment, he had a photocopy of the codicil. He also knew the great story here was not the codicil itself but what mayhem the codicil would produce—particularly in Las Vegas.

He did what every honest citizen would do.

He'd turn the document over to the IRS.

Now the story was reporting what the IRS was doing about a document it had received alleging a $50 million codicil by a man long dead. As long as he didn't print his copy of the codicil, he had a lock on the story.

Then he went one better.

These were bastards who had been auditing him for years.

He'd show them.

He wrote up a front-page article on the codicil, with the bold headline **"WE'LL LOOK INTO IT!"** and credited the quote to George O'Brien, Senior IRS Auditor. He had the title correct because he had secured O'Brien's business card at the center of the dartboard in his office. O'Brien had been and was the IRS auditor who had been plumbing the accounts of the *Las Vegas Scandal, Inc.* for years. Otterburg had complained that the IRS was harassing the *Las Vegas Scandal, Inc.* because it was small and the other Las Vegas papers had large circulations. O'Brien's response had been that if Otterburg ever had any charges to make and the documents to back up those charges, "We'll look into it."

O'Brien had made the quote, so Otterburg placed O'Brien's name and title—in slightly smaller print—immediately beneath the blazing headline. After all, Otterburg had a charge to make and the document to back up those charge. So, certainly, the IRS was going to look into "it." The definition of "it" might be different from O'Brien's perspective, but O'Brien had said it, so it was up to the IRS auditor—identified as such on the front page of *Las Vegas Scandal, Inc.*—to explain "it" to the other newspapers and television stations in Las Vegas. If the drunk was correct, at the end of the day there was only one person besides the IRS who had a photocopy of the codicil: Walter Otterburg, publisher/editor/ reporter for *Las Vegas Scandal, Inc.*

He sent a copy of the tabloid by registered mail to the director of the Las Vegas office of the IRS.

Wednesday night.

With guaranteed delivery on Thursday morning.

Just to show proof that he had contacted the IRS, at the bottom of the front page he had included a scan of the registered mail receipt to the director of the Las Vegas office of the IRS by registered mail IRS.

He also put a thank-you note to George O'Brien, along with a dozen copies of the tabloid, and personally delivered the envelope the Las Vegas IRS office.

Thursday afternoon.

At 3:00 p.m.

Half an hour later, he made a few select calls to Las Vegas television stations, newspapers, and tabloids. Did they know that a Howard Hughes codicil had popped up? No? Well, the IRS is "looking into it." Could they see the codicil? Well, no, actually. It *was quite possible* that it would be the centerpiece of a legal dispute and the *last thing* Otterburg wanted was legal trouble with the IRS. (Perish the thought!)

But he could FAX them a copy of the front page of the most recent *Las Vegas Scandal, Inc.* that would be on the streets in a few hours. It had front-page proof that the IRS had been sent the codicil. They might want to give the IRS a call and ask for a comment.

CHAPTER 4

ARCHIE ZELITHE SCARBOROUGH

On every first day of his class on American history, Archie Zelithe Scarborough, known as "Prof" to his student, passed out a copy of the *Business Insider* with its article on economics studies. The October 7, 2015, article highlighted the testing of economic studies by two Federal Reserve economists who determined that two-thirds of all published, reputable economic studies in nationally recognized economics journals could not be replicated.

In street language, they jimmied the results.

That was a pretty poor track record, Prof would say. Here in Las Vegas, he would say each semester, these are the kind of numbers you bet *against.*

This, Prof always said, should come as no surprise. Students, he advised, should keep in mind that economics was an academic field whose basic principle was that all people are rational and will always choose to buy the best product at the best price. That, he noted, was a myth. If all people were rational all the time, there would be no need of the study of economics.

Or history, for that matter.

31

But not all people are rational and reasonable, and, therefore, unpredictable. "Remember," he would continually tell his students, "history is not the story of the past; it is a study of the future. If you want to know what *is going* to happen, look *at what has* happened. We keep making the same foolish mistakes time after time after time. Any time you think you've heard of the stupidest thing a person can do, just wait a week."

Las Vegas, Prof told his students, was a city founded on dreams—and cons. Nothing had changed. It was still a city of dreams. It was still a city where con jobs were standards. The first non-Native to arrive in the Las Vegas area was a Mexican scout by the name of Rafael Rivera. He took stock of "the meadows," the translation of "Las Vegas," a name that stuck. The area also had an abundant supply of water, crucial to the establishment of a settlement. It had the water then, snidely remarked Prof, "not so much now." Then the meadows and waters were free—in the middle of a desert. That, if nothing else, was a traveler's dream come true.

The first large-scale con was in 1844 when a dubious war hero by the name of John C. Frémont wrote that Las Vegas was an excellent place for settlement. Frémont was one of those people who would have fit in well with the Las Vegas of today, Prof would say. Frémont was a smooth talker, pushed the limits of his authority beyond all bounds, and was able to s-l-i-d-e through the system because he was married to the daughter of the most powerful U.S. Senator of the era. His wife, Jessie, was the daughter of Senator Thomas Hart Benton of Missouri.

Senator Benton, from Tennessee, had been an aide-de-camp to Gen. Andrew Jackson and had been assigned the political job of s-m-o-o-t-h-i-n-g things for Jackson in Washington, DC, during the War of 1812. This should have done wonders for Benton's career. He was personally connected to the most popular man in America, who was on his way to becoming the president of the United States. Benton had been promoted to lieutenant colonel and had high-level political contacts in Washington, DC. Then, on a fluke, he had become involved in a duel against his mentor. Jackson was wounded, and that ended the relationship.

But wait!

This was American history, Prof would say in his class.

Nothing in American history is as it seems.

After being involved with the duel, Benton *left* Tennessee for newly acquired Missouri Territory. He set up a law practice in St. Louis but quickly fell into his old ways. During a court case in 1817, he and the opposing lawyer, Charles Lucas, exchanged words that led to an exchange of curses, charges and countercharges, and, as such things ended in those days, a duel. In those days, duels were held on Bloody Island. The island was little more than a sandbar, which was densely wooded. It was the ideal place for a duel, as it was in the Mississippi River, which was the boundary between the territories of both Missouri and Illinois. So Bloody Island *was not* in Missouri or Illinois.

In the first duel—there were two—between Benton and Lucas, Benton's knee was grazed by a bullet. Lucas was not so lucky. He took a slug in his throat. Benton was talked out of taking a second shot, a fatal one, and both men went their separate ways.

For a while.

Until Lucas healed.

Then Lucas challenged Benton to *another* duel.

He should have kept his mouth shut.

This time—in the same year on the same island—Benton shot Lucas dead.

The duel did nothing to lower the esteem of Benton to the population of settlers in the Missouri Territory. When Missouri became a state in 1820, Benton was one of its first senators. He would serve in the United States Senate representing Missouri for 30 years, the first man to serve that long in the United States Senate. During eight of those years, 1828–1836, the President of the United States was the man with whom Benton had been across the cross hairs in a duel: Andrew Jackson.

What made Benton and his son-in-law Frémont a good match—aside from Jessie—was that both were hard-core expansionists. Both men wanted to see the United States stretch from sea to shining sea, with every single square foot between the two in American hands. The two were hand in glove, with Benton authoring the first Homestead Act to give "free" land to encourage settlement and Frémont writing books on his expeditions to the Far West and—most importantly— drawing maps that highlighted which trails to use to get there. "There," in the case of Frémont, were many places where he would eventually own land.

It was on Frémont's third expedition to California that he fell afoul of Washington, DC. On this expedition, he was ordered to locate the source of the Arkansas River. The source of the river was believed to be somewhere in what is now the state of Colorado. Suddenly, without explanation—and without orders—Frémont changed his directive and headed for California. Arriving in 1846 in advance of the Mexican-American War, he began to stir up the American settlers in the Sacramento area. He *suggested* that since a war with Mexico was about to break out—California then being a part of Mexico—his troops were there to protect the settlers from the Mexican army. When the Mexican-American War did break out two years later, the American settlers established an independent republic, the Bear Flag Republic. Frémont, who had previously told the same American settlers that he was there to protect them, then used his army to seize control of the Bear Flag Republic and declare himself the military governor of California.

That was too much for the president of the United States, James K. Polk. Frémont was court-martialed and ordered to return to Washington, DC.

Was Frémont going to be convicted of mutiny when his father-in-law was the most powerful U.S. senator?

Welcome to politics America style!

Frémont was not only exonerated but also had led two more military expeditions into the Far West. He was also elected as one of the first two U.S. senators from California and, oddly, as the fifth territorial governor of Arizona—until he was forced to resign because he did not bother to show up for work. Though he had acquired substantial acres of land in California—some of the land claims having to be settled by the U.S. Supreme Court—Frémont died broke in 1890.

All this being said, the tag team of Benton and Frémont radically changed the Far West generally and what would become Las Vegas specifically. Senator Benton pushed westward expansion hard in the halls of Congress, while his son-in-law did the exploring and—of critical importance to Las Vegas—produced the maps that were to be used by the settlers coming west. Frémont's books and maps sold very well—and were of particular interest to the Mormons. Because of nationwide animosity toward the Mormons, they had been hopscotching from community to community, heading further and further west every time they were *asked* to leave a local. They finally made the decision to move to what is now Utah and Salt Lake City.

When it came to business, the Mormons were no slouches. They understood the value of raw land and proceeded to grab as much of it as fast as they could while it was still free. To this end they established Mormon settlements across the Great Basin and as far west as San Francisco and Los Angeles. Their timing could not have been better. The Treaty of Guadalupe-Hidalgo ended the war with Mexico and put the ownership of the land in the Great Basin in transition. It had been Mexican then and now it was American. If the Mormons moved fast, they could claim a substantial chunk for themselves and eventually establish a state within the United States. A Mormon state they could not be *asked* to leave. To this end they established the Territory of Deseret, which included all the land between the Rocky and the Sierra Nevada mountains as far north as Canada and as far south as Mexico. If it had been admitted as a state, it would have included large portions of what is now California, Arizona, Utah, Nevada, New Mexico, Colorado, Wyoming, Idaho, and Oregon.

It didn't happen.

When the United States established the Territory of Utah in 1850, the dream of a state of Deseret died.

But this did not stop the Mormons. They would continue to establish settlements wherever the acreage was free, water was available, and the land fertile. In places like Las Vegas. In 1855, courtesy of the maps created by Frémont, the Mormons established a fort in what

35

would become Las Vegas. Conveniently located midway between Salt Lake City and Los Angeles, it was designed as a watering hole and way station for Mormons on their way to the Pacific Coast and for cargo trains of food and supplies from Los Angeles to make their way to Salt Lake City.

The Mormons were not in Las Vegas very long, and it would be half a century before Las Vegas would be reborn—this time as a railroad town. A growing community was established in 1905 when the Union Pacific Railroad came through. Now, with a transportation link to the outside world, the free land became valuable. Cargo that had previously been considered in pounds was now being shipped in tons. The modern city sank its roots into the desert sand when 110 acres were auctioned off, and in 1911, the city was incorporated. It remained a fly spec on the map of Nevada until the Great Depression. In 1931, to drive up instate income, Nevada legalized gambling and allowed couples who wanted a quickie divorce to get one in Nevada with six weeks' residency. The construction of the Hoover Dam brought thousands of workers to Las Vegas in that decade, and they spent their money in the only nearby town: Las Vegas. When World War II started, a gunnery school was established nearby, and when the war ended, nuclear testing and the creation of the infamous Area 51 sucked highly paid federal employees into Las Vegas like light into a black hole.

Historically speaking, Prof told his classes, the formation of Las Vegas *then* is just like *today*. Las Vegas is discovered, and the population goes up. People get tired of it and leave. The population goes down. A new industry arrives, and the population bounces up again. Even more important, every time the population increases, the city extends further out across the desert. When the population leaves, homes go into default, and businesses close their doors.

Until the next industry boom moves in.

Then the old homes are refitted, remodeled, and refinanced, and as the boom continues, the city, again, moves further and further out into the desert. Year by new industry by next boom, the city's outskirts pulse out and then, with the inevitable recession, contract.

Historically and today, everything in Las Vegas is a gamble. Benton and Frémont gambled they could extend the borders of the United States with a coordinated effort of Benton in Congress and with Frémont's maps in the hands of settlers. The Mormons gambled they could hold the fort on the trail between Salt Lake City and Los Angeles. The Union Pacific Railroad gambled it could make money carrying passengers into Las Vegas and tons of cargo through Las Vegas to markets on the East and West Coast. Today, Las Vegas is betting that it will remain the premier American gambling location and survive offshore betting, onshore computer poker, fantasy football, and online porn. "So far, Las Vegas has a winning hand," Prof told his class. "But keep in mind that every hour of every day, there is someone and groups of someones who are looking at the odds of success at some con game. Be it cards or roulette, horse racing or land speculation, there is always someone betting they can beat the system. Maybe they can, who knows? After all, this is *Las Vegas!*"

CHAPTER 5

JEAN "ZAPATA" PETERS

The only thing Elizabeth Jean Peters had in common with Jean Elizabeth Peters was that both dropped the name Elizabeth. That was the extent of their connection. The former had been married to Howard Hughes and the latter had never been married at all. They were also different; in that, the former was a movie star of sparkling talent, who eschewed becoming a sex symbol; the latter worked overtime for the opposite effect.

The daughter of a modestly successful Las Vegas Realtor and his partner/secretary/wife, the Jean Peters who was not Howard Hughes's wife was known in high school as "Zapata" because the other Jean Peters was burning up the screen in *Viva Zapata!* That was the high school freshman year of the Jean Peters who had never been married to Howard Hughes. The nickname stuck and so did many of the on-screen mannerism she adopted from her onscreen namesake.

There the similarities ended.

By the time Elizabeth Jean Peters married Howard Hughes in 1957, Zapata was on the street in Las Vegas. A downtick in the real-estate market had swallowed her parents' business without so much as a burp. Her mother had died of breast cancer the year before, and her father had married a show girl, who didn't know an acre from an archway. What the real-estate market had not taken from her father, the show girl did. He died of alcoholism in a sanitarium in Hemet; the show girl absconded with everything in the home that was loose, and the house in which Zapata had been living went back to the bank.

When it comes to real estate in Las Vegas, the term *demise* is a grotesque misnomer. Unlike other cities in America, the Las Vegas real-estate frontier does not grow, contract, or expand. It pulses. In other communities there is a business core—usually called downtown—and the residential market oozes out in all directions. Freeways stretch like the arms of a concrete octopus into the suburbs, and houses rise from the vineyard and orange groves like warriors born of dragon's teeth.

Until there is downturn in the economy.

Then the houses gradually lose their value until the economy rebounds and then the established houses return to their pre-recession prices, and the city expands outward again, taking advantage of the unceasing reach of those concrete octopus arms of the freeways.

Las Vegas, however, is different. When the economy turns bad, and houses are abandoned, the land beneath the foreclosed property is now cheap enough for low-end malls. Shopping centers rise from the ashes of the abandoned suburbs. Then, as the economy recovers, the land beneath the malls become more valuable for high-end houses, and the low-end malls are supplanted by luxury subdivisions. Then new, more modern malls are built further out, which stimulates the extension of the water, sewer, and electrical network lines that, in turn, stimulates the construction of low-end subdivisions. Then, inevitably, there will be a downturn in the economy, and the low-end houses will be abandoned. Now the land will be cheap enough for the rise of more modern malls, shopping centers, and plazas, along with high-end homes, and the real-estate pulsing continues.

Zapata's parents' real-estate business was a casualty of this entrepreneurial cycle. Worse, they had the misfortune to be located close to what came to be called the Strip. At the end of the Second World War, it was simply a shoulder-to-shoulder line of small businesses, each leaning drunkenly against its neighbor. There were pawnshops next to the hole-in-the-wall gambling halls beside saloons, with the inevitable greasy spoons shuffled in between. Bugsy Siegel tried to inject life into the Strip, but he got his in Los Angeles in the summer of 1947. Nothing much happened until the very early 1950s, just as Zapata was entering high school. Until then, the big money in Las Vegas was being made because of the nuclear testing. That brought lots of government workers to town, and the real-estate market started to twitch.

The Teamsters Union Pension Fund came to town shortly thereafter, and big-name casinos exploded out of the desert sands. The Sands, Sahara, Showboat, and Rivera showed the ghost of Bugsy how to do it right. The right way was to combine casinos going up with top-of-the-line performers coming in. Eight million people a year were beating feet to the Strip to see the stars of stage and film who were known worldwide just by their first names: Elvis, Liberace, Dean, Frank, Andy, Bob, and Bing. Each attracted their own gaggle of ticket buyers—which increased yearly—a gift that kept on giving as children brought by their parents grew up and brought their grandchildren. The Strip was a gift that kept giving, a juggernaut of cash that showed no signs of slowing, much less stopping.

But it did stop the small realtors like the Peters. They were swallowed and were lucky if they could get their furniture out the back door as the wrecking ball was coming in the front.

Within a decade, downtown Las Vegas was wall-to-wall casinos, gourmet restaurants, high-end fashion stores, out-of-this-world hair salons, and from-the-far-ends-of-the-universe jewelry stores.

Life was very good along the Strip. It wasn't too bad if you were living in the actual city of Las Vegas. The high life and gambling were the heartbeat of the Strip, but a dozen blocks back in the actual city of Las Vegas, you could not tell it was a city of lights. The further away from the Strip you lived, the more life was "normal." With the exception of the Strip, it was a middle-class city with banks, mortgage companies, restaurants, supermarkets, health club and the like. You could live ten blocks back from the Strip and never know it was there—unless a nightclub entertainer or card dealer lived next door. For the most part, Las Vegas was not the Strip and the Strip was not Las Vegas.

But the Strip was where Zapata had to make her living. By the time she was out of high school, her parents' business was gone. Her father had managed to pay for her to spend two part-time semesters at a junior college, but that money ran out when his second wife did. So, at 20, she was on her own. But this was not all bad news. She was 20 in 1955, and Las Vegas was about to howl! Elvis, Frank, Bing, and Bob were in town along with eight million tourists a year. She found a job as a card dealer—which was not hard for the locals in those days—and settled into a career path in the casino business.

That lasted a little more than a decade. In 1966, just as Howard Hughes was making his entrance, Zapata was going out the door.

CHAPTER 6

LAS VEGAS POLITE DEPARTMENT

Jerry Kemp did not really work for the Las Vegas *Police* Department. He worked for the Las Vegas *Polite* Department. He was the pleasant face of law enforcement. It was a fraud and a crock, but someone had to do it. Someone had to be the nice guy, the avuncular fellow who soothed things over. There were the cops on beat who dealt with the gangs. There were the traffic cops who gave out the tickets. There were the community cops who handled the broke gamblers who ordered a meal but could not pay for it. He was the cop who handled the celebrities who believed they were God's gift to mankind. You could not live with them, and you could not kill them. They had what was quietly called Las Vegas immunity. Until they pulled a gun, they could pretty much do what they wanted. But someone had to clean up the messes. That someone was Jerry Kemp.

Kemp was off the Sunday that Dobbins was arrested. When he came in Monday morning and read the police report about the arrest, all he could do was shake his head in disbelief and roll his eyes. Talk about sending boys to do a man's job. Talk about racking up the I-hate-cops points by cooperating with the IRS, a *federal* agency. Talk about ignoring and thus upsetting the press for no reason whatsoever. This kind of a high-profile arrest was going to have repercussions.

His day got even worse when he saw the headlines of the morning newspaper.

Newspapers.

All of them.

The circus was in town.

It was going to be a long day.

CHAPTER 7

JEREMY "JIGGER" MOONEY

Jeremy Mooney had not started out in life to be banker. He had not started to be anything but employed. He did not have numbers in blood, so to speak, or, for that matter, in his dreams. His dreams were strictly pornographic. But that was as far as it went. In his early days, he had not the money to indulge in his fantasy passions. When he settled into his day job with a wife and stepchild, he could not afford to be the man about town he wanted to be. Even after the divorce, his life followed such a parsimonious path that he could not afford to satisfy his inner cravings.

After a stint in the U.S. army, wasting four years of his life in Germany and Virginia, he came home and got a job as a bartender in a dying section of Cleveland. There, on a seedy street in the "Mistake on the Lake," he was the last bartender in town. That's not to say that there were no other men and women who served liquor by the snifter, decanter, or goblet. There were. But they were not "bartenders," as he liked to say. They were simply dispensers of liquid refreshment.

That was all.

They were not bartenders.

A bartender was not simply a mixologist. He was not just a purveyor of exotic drinks either. In a word, a bartender was a confidant. A true bartender was both a listener and dispenser of sage advice. More important than that, he was the living history of his patrons.

The generic dispensers of liquid refreshment, on the other hand, were only masters—and mistresses—of the blender and soda gun. Yes, they could create any concoction known to man, woman, or the recipe book they happened to have under the counter or in the keg room. Whether it was a Cosmopolitan or bloody mary, Sloe Screw or Bourbon and branch, they knew their stuff the way the equipment manager of a major league baseball team knew his inventory by length, width, and wood type. But they were more like jukeboxes: drop in 35 cents, and the automaton will play any song for which there was a record. But don't ask what to do about an ailing wife or a supervisor with a bad streak of passive-aggressive behavior.

There were, he often said, two kinds of drinking establishments. The first, most popular, was the nightclub. It did not have an ebb and flow of customers; just a tide. The term "regular" had very little meaning, as the patrons were simply the gift of the economy. They came with their company credit cards and remained until they had somewhere better to go, up the company food chain or into a trophy marriage. Customers arrived, stayed for an indeterminate stretch of time, and left, never to be seen again.

The second kind of drinking establishment were called the bars. He used the term with no sense of derision. He was a bartender. He worked in a bar. The American bar—not to be confused with the legal profession, though many of the latter found refreshment from the former—was an institution as old as America itself. The Pilgrims had landed where they did because they were running short of beer, a fact he underlined in the almanac he kept behind the counter. "We could not now take time for further search for a place to land," recorded one bibulous Pilgrim on the **Mayflower**, "as our victuals being much spent, especially our beer."

In Cleveland he was known as the "Nigger with the Jigger" and thereafter simply Jigger. He had been the fixture bartender at the Twisted

45

Lemon for two decades, and he was also going to be the last, as there was a fleet of bulldozers gathering like a band of Indians in war paint at the end of the street. Every once in a while, one of the iron beasts would kick into life and lever its maw up and down as if to remind the denizens of the Twisted Lemon, the last operating establishment for three blocks, that progress was inevitable and destruction near.

The demise of the Twisted Lemon had been ordained in the stars. It was an institution and establishment frozen in amber. It had opened as a neighborhood watering hole when the terms "neighborhood" and "bar" were positive in both the denotative and connotative. In 1932, when some nameless purveyor of liquid drink poured his first shot, the Twisted Lemon was smack-dab in the center of a respectable neighborhood, three blocks from an elementary school and the same distance from a meat market. There were no grocery stores in those days. They were a neighborhood creature of the next decade. In the 1930s, you got your meat from a butcher, your bread from a bread shop, vegetables from the market—which was really an open-air market where the farmers came every Saturday and Sunday to sell their produce—including sweets from the DULCE, the store where Jigger's soon-to-be wife was working, and it was she who got him the job at the Twisted Lemon in 1965. Jigger had been unemployed at the time, debating whether to go back into the mindless ranks of the military or seek his fortune elsewhere. There were not a lot of elsewheres to go in those days if you did not have a college degree, so he took the job.

When he got married, his life changed instantly. He went from a cot in the back of his uncle's warehouse to a double bed in the back room of a squalid rooming house with a pregnant wife whose mother spoke only Italian and father spoke to Jigger in a mixture of Polish with English and Italian.

The old man hadn't needed English. He supervised the loading crew for a meat-market chain, a good job for an immigrant. The old man had gotten the job because the one language he did not speak well was English. But he didn't need to speak English. His daughter did it for him and only when there was a problem. The rest of the time, he spoke

Polish, German, French, and Italian to the immigrants who lugged the beeves bodies out of the railway cars and hung them on the meat hooks in the truck trailers for delivery to the dozen Callahan meat markets on the south side of the city.

The old man was massive in girth but short in stature, about five feet tall. That was about the same distance from the right index fingertip to the left. He needed his muscle because not all the immigrants understood that the beeves they were offloading belonged to the Callahan meat markets. There was no skim here. Not with Andrzej on the dock— "Andrew" to the sellers in the Callahan meat markets and on his checks that his wife picked up and deposited every Friday at noon so that the old man would not spend too much at the Twisted Lemon, then without a bartender.

Jigger's mother-in-law, Amalia, was from Boston, the daughter of a somewhat prosperous fruit merchant who had run afoul of the local constabulary. Amalia had been sent west to Cleveland to keep her out of the mess that sent her father to the penitentiary. He was last seen on a train headed south to Florida, where he expected to make millions on some scam-involving land, with a handful of characters of mixed ethnic heritage he had befriended in prison—or they had befriended him, the story was unclear to Amalia. But it did not matter because the old man was never heard from again.

Amalia's first marriage was to an Italian, the son of an ice-cream and cake-shop owner. The shop had changed its name to DULCE during the First World War, so there would be no hint of Italian involvement, but that turned out to be a bad choice. Twenty years later, the name of the shop and the leader of the Italian fascist nation were but a letter apart. Amalia's husband died young, and she remarried, this time to a man who was as honest as the day was long and regular as the sunrise. They were happy together and argued in four languages. After she took up with Andrzej, they had a daughter, Rosa.

Rosa grew up with DULCE. It was a family business, and Rosa learned the ropes—or, at least, the confections—from an early age. She also married at an early age, to a Polish man twice as old as she was. The

47

marriage was actually a business transaction—of sorts. The Pole brought to the wedding the funding necessary to double the size of the shop. When the agreed-upon child was born—days before Jigger and Rosa were married—the loan was considered paid off, and the first marriage annulled by an understanding Italian cleric from upstate. Rosa was then richer by one son and was the bona fide half owner of DULCE with her mother. Jigger was thus her second husband. That was a marriage made in both heaven and the First Bank of Chicago. Jigger was a hard worker who had saved a modest chunk of his army pay. He also spoke enough Polish to keep his father-in-law happy.

Jigger had needed no interview to be employed at the Twisted Lemon. The owner was a remote cousin of Andrzej, and a Pole's word was good among Poles. So Jigger began working at the Twisted Lemon immediately after the birth of Rosa's child.

The next day.

There was no honeymoon, since Rosa had just completed childbirth. Then followed six tumultuous years with Jigger honing his skills as a bartender and caring for a growing, disreputable son who proved it was possible to go from 6 to 13 with none of the intervening years. The lad was also racially conflicted, as he believed he was not Italian, Polish, black, or American. Of what ethic strain he was, he never stated but hung around in the Irish and German neighborhoods on either side of the Little Italy and New Poland street that divided the neighborhoods. The son was eventually to find a term that identified him perfectly: felon. After the trial, he was known by another: inmate. The first of these he kept for life, as short as it was. The second was for a stretch of five to ten, of which he served seven and was later found in the shallows of the nearby river. He had apparently tried to swim while wrapped in 30 feet of heavy gauge chain. As there was no sign of violence, and the police had more than enough murders to investigate, the boy was listed as a suicide, and that, as they said in Cleveland in those years, was the end of that.

Jigger had no trouble-making friends, and this was a blessing because in the bartendering business, particularly in the days when most bars were neighborhood establishments, it did not do to upset the regular clientele. What made the Twisted Lemon so unusual, and undoubtedly the reason it survived as long as it did, was that it serviced a wide ethnic swath of the community, including Poles, Germans, Irish, blacks, some wandering Jews, Lithuanians, Bohunks, and assorted others of European stock. This was a blessing because the Twisted Lemon did not turn into an ethnic enclave. It was a neighborhood bar, and it reflected the changing cultural makeup of the neighborhood at whatever moment in history one wished to discuss. It started Eastern European and ended Mexican with black and yellow in-between.

As the years wore on, Jigger came to realize that while he was a master of the alcoholic liquid, there was a very dark downside to the profession. While he treated his wife as an equal—which she was—he was serving clients of many cultures who looked upon their wives as property. Chattel would have been a better term, a word Jigger had to look up when a Balkan learning English used the word. He had said his wife was *chattel* and, by God, that was the way he treated her. She wasn't good enough to just be beaten; she had to be pounded. That was the way you got women to understand their place in the real world, the Balkan had said. Chattel. The Balkan liked that word.

This was nothing new to Jigger. As culture after culture wafted through the Twisted Lemon, he heard the same thing from the Italians, Germans, Mexicans, Spaniards, Japanese, Chinese, whites, and blacks. Women were property. If this was all there was to the attitude, Jigger might have been able to accept it as a reality of the world that he was living.

But this was not the case.

Considering a wife as chattel was simply the first step down into a very dark cellar. Alcohol made an angry man dangerous. The men who came to the Twisted Lemon were not those who knew their limits. If they had, they would have been drinking at home. The men who patronized the Twisted Lemon were hard-core drinkers. They only stopped when they ran out of money and credit. Then they became unruly, surly, and combative. They went home and took out their frustration with the dead-end life they were living on their wives. On many more than one occasion, Jigger let wives spend the night in the closed Twisted Lemon because they were bleeding badly from fisticuffs and had no other place to go. It would not be any better for them come morning, but at least for that night they were safe.

If this had been the extent of his brush with the dark side of alcohol, he could have continued with his Pollyanna view of the industry. But alcoholism is a progressive disease as is domestic violence. Neither are limited by law, culture, or good sense. On far more than a dozen nights a year, the Twisted Lemon saw examples of both to the point that each was considered a by-product of human existence. None of the patrons thought that coldcocking was anything out of the ordinary. Child abuse was standard as well. Again, on far more than a dozen times, Jigger had watched a bruised child grow up to be an abused wife or abusing husband. It was a cycle to destruction that, again, was not limited by law, culture, or good sense.

While Jigger had been a heavy drinker in the army, he sobered as a bartender. He, as well as his customers, was married to a dead-end job. The only difference was that Jigger knew there was something better for him down the road. He did not know when his ship was going to come in, so to speak; he just had to make sure he was on the right dock at the right time when the ocean liner docked. He also had to be sober when the ship tied up at the wharf. At the beginning of his second decade in the Twisted Lemon, he gave up alcohol. He still served it, but he just didn't drink it.

Through his two decades at the Twisted Lemon, Jigger was as steady as the grandfather's clock that leaned against the wainscot in the corner between where the bar ended and the restrooms began. It had been a pawn of a sailor who had come through town with a greater thirst than his paycheck would allow and had squandered his father's inheritance, such as it was, between the deceased man's apartment and the river. Every bar in the area ended up with some furniture. When the sailor had thus extinguished his father's largess, he went back to sea. He never came back, and the grandfather's clock, a bit warped from its years in an apartment that had a leaking ceiling, sat in the Twisted Lemon reverently chiming every quarter hour. Oiled every six months, it kept time as long as its pendulum kept rocking, and its weights were pulled back to the top of the clock every seven to ten days. In the 35 years it had been in the Twisted Lemon, it had only stopped once, and that was when Jigger and Rosa had gone on a belated honeymoon to Atlantic City, as far as the blushing bride had gone in her married life. When they had returned, the clock had stopped because the Bohunk substitute barman had taken his two weeks' wages from the first night's receipts and left town for parts unknown. This had been the only two weeks in its existence the Twisted Lemon was locked up.

Odd it was that the clock should have stopped at that instant. It was as if it knew its life was extinguishing and that the moment had come for it to expire and allow its enumerated soul to speed off to the never-never land of timepieces. It simply gave up the chronological ghost. During the week that Jigger and Rosa had been gone, the bulldozers had begun their inevitable razing at the far end of the street. They were halfway to DULCE within a fortnight, and the Twisted Lemon went the way of all things with one exception: instead of dust to dust, it went from timber-and-nails to dust. In the end it did not matter, as it was gone from this world.

More than shingles and boards went into the dust heap of the Twisted Lemon and DULCE. Twenty years of marriage went as well. Rosa wanted to stay in Cleveland and open a new DULCE with her family. Jigger was tired of snow and wind and in-laws. The divorce was amiable, with Rosa moving uptown and Jigger flying west. He made it as far as Las Vegas, where he got a job as a night bartender in the Bullion Lounge. The job would have lasted as long as he was able to stand the clientele, but he had his eyes set for the future. He was tired of mixing drinks and all the human problems that came from the demon rum. He knew very well the road well traveled when it came to alcohol, and he knew he was better off standing on trackside rather than boarding the Bourbon express.

The Lord works in mysterious ways.

Now, as a midnight-to-8:00 a.m. purveyor of liquid refreshment in an establishment with no regulars—and not as the true bartender he used

51

to be—an unexpected advantage came his way. He could go to college during the day and take business classes with a banking emphasis. Of the little that he knew beyond the bar business, education was his ticket out. So he boarded the train.

Luck favors the audacious.

It was in the banking classes that Jigger came to understand the truth of the adage that "everyone makes their own luck." He had seen proof of this dictum in his life but only in the negative. As a bartender, he had seen the consequences of an action as trivial as passing a rumor. The ill someone spoke had a tendency to come back and bite them in the trouser back pockets. Time and time again he had seen the consequences of the cycle of retribution. What he had yet to learn was that there was flipside to the cycle: it was cyclical as well. It was just a lot longer for the good to cycle back around.

For decades, were not for bad luck, he would have had no luck at all. Las Vegas turned out to be quite different. That was because Las Vegas was built on luck. You struck it rich in Las Vegas by making your own luck, and that did not mean at the gaming table. Rather, Las Vegas was a land of luck in the sense that opportunities were there for the taking. You had to work hard in the taking, but it was not like being in Cleveland where the ethnics had long since bottled up every gravy train on every track. In Las Vegas, if you did not like what was going on, all you had to do was wait a week, and everything would be changed. New faces replaced the old, new schemes supplanted the old ones, and the lights never went dim.

Jigger wanted something better than bartending. So he began taking business classes at the local junior college. Thus did his life change dramatically. First and foremost, he was an oddity in his business classes. He was well into his forties and had more than two decades in the bar business. While he did not have the academic background of the rest of the students, he could read people like a book. His fellow students might just as well have poked through goat entrails to predict the future, while Jigger could see a con job a block and a half away in a sandstorm.

Several of his instructors were retired bankers who knew exactly what they were seeing. In Jigger, they recognized a rare talent. They jiggled the credit mill to get him quarter units for time served as an "entertainment entrepreneur"—which was significant in Las Vegas where everyone was in the entertainment business. He received OJT units as well as an internship that put him into the Rutherford Bank and Trust, a modest establishment that primarily catered to the unique needs of casinos on and off the Strip. He was able to leap over the State of Nevada, Department of Banking and Securities' *suggested* requirement of six months of management training. He landed on his feet and in the chair of the retiring manager of Casino Transactions. His job was primarily to handle the incoming cash from the casinos and secondarily—and more importantly—to keep an eagle eye alert for the one-a-day schemes, scams, and cons that waterfalls of cash naturally generate. His income went up by a factor of four, and for the first time in his life, he owned a car.

But just as Jigger could see the schemes and scams coming down the sidewalk, he quickly came to understand the arcane machinations within the bank itself. There was no edge of the law in banking, simply the whim of the regulators who were far away from the auditors who regularly and superficially examined the bank's books. As long as there was not a pterodactyl hiding in the debits, the bank would get a clean bill of health.

What Jigger also learned quickly was that there was no such thing as a violation of the laws in banking. It was a concept that did not exist. Robbing a bank with a pistol was a felony; doing the same with a pen made you a vice-president. As a consequence, what would be considered a financial violation of the law in business was a reality of the banking world. The only limit was what regulators would allow, and there were neither enough regulators to go around nor the administrative backbone to enforce what antiquated regulations that were on the books gathering dust in some bureaucrats' offices in far-off Washington, DC. Little wonder, there was a banking meltdown in 2008, and since then nothing had happened. Bankers were still skylarking with federal moneys, and no one inside or outside of the industry seemed to give a tinker's damn.

The rule of thumb in the Las Vegas banking industry—and most likely across all state lines—was simply not to draw undue attention to any practice. It was better to beg forgiveness than ask permission, and the banks shouldered the line of acceptance until a regulator did a tsk-tsk-tsk. Thereafter, the bank did not abandon the process; it just adjusted the vocabulary. "Bad debt" could become a "business loss," which, as far as income tax liability was concerned, was the same thing, but, to banking auditor, in different columns and therefore different accounts.

Jigger was a blessing to Rutherford Bank and Trust because he saw and understood the financial gyrations but made no comment. This allowed the bank to expand his sphere of influence into mortgages oversight where the real money moved. You can steal more with a pen than a gun, and, in banking lexicography, the term "steal" is defined as what regulators will not allow. As long as the pterodactyls went undiscovered, all was well.

CHAPTER 8

HAROLD CHARLES DOBBINS IN JAIL

Dobbins was hardly a man of the world. He was not a man of the streets either. He was, if nothing else, one of those boring individuals to whom accounting is exciting. This is not to say that he found life in columns of numbers or told jokes about accountants. It was that he had a sense of satisfaction when he chased $.16 for an hour and finally found it so he could drag it into the correct column of numbers on a sheet of the same in a report of the same that was filed in some cabinet, with reams of the same to be examined by state and federal regulators whose life was as fulfilling as Dobbins. He had no sense of humor. His persona had no highs or lows, simply the low-level hum of existence like the sound a radio makes between stations. He was the epitome of the one and only joke regarding accountants: the difference between a computer and an accountant is that the computer has a personality.

There were, Dobbins knew, very few accounting jokes. The biggest problem was that accountants do not laugh, so no one is ever sure the accountant appreciated the joke, understood the humor therein, or it was a waste of valuable time that could have been spent adding up columns

55

of number. Alas, if you are an accountant, it is an accrual world, but, at the very least, you are in a department where everyone counts. Homeless accountants live in tax shelters and suffer from depreciation. The only four things accountants know for sure is that trial balances do not, bank reconciliations never do, working capital does not, and returns on investment never will.

It was this lack of a sense of humor that made his stay in the Las Vegas jail doubly hard; he had no columns to reconcile. But his stay was going to be short because he knew that there was no way anyone could find real money that did not exist. Even more important, the amount was so great that there was no way it could have slipped through the accounting cracks—of which there were few known and none invented—and escape state and federal auditors for half a century—not to mention the IRS and the FBI.

If there was a silver lining to his tale of woe, it was that he was in the Las Vegas city jail. This was a local holding facility, neither state nor federal. This meant he was a low-level risk. It also meant that no one was absolutely, positively sure he had something to hide. He knew from experience that the Las Vegas Police Department was subject to political pressure. What this meant in the real world was that the servants of law and order would run you in if someone "up the administrative food chain" wanted to "jerk your chain." Someone would be picked up on a bogus charge and kept a few days while the paperwork "got lost" or wound its way up to someone with an IQ who said the case smelled like a skunk in a closet—or, euphemistically, in the terms of a legal beagle, "had no merit"—and you were released.

Dobbins was not stupid.

He knew there was a lot more going on here than just the bogus codicil.

He just didn't know what it was.

But here he was, sitting in a Las Vegas city jail, yet the charges against him were federal. Actually, there were no charges. He was being held as a material witness. That was why the IRS had shown up at his door first. His arrest—or, as the authorities were wiggling the words around to say, his *detention*—was because he was a material witness. But the arrest was made by the Las Vegas police. So he was being *detained* on a city warrant. That made no sense at all. A federal charge should have meant arrest—or *detention*—by federal authorities. So why wasn't the FBI involved? If not the FBI, why not another federal law-enforcement agency? Didn't the IRS have a law-enforcement arm, a department that arrested people? The IRS could subpoena records; could they arrest people as well? If it could, why hadn't his detention been made by that department? If there was a federal charge, why wasn't he in a federal lockup?

At the very least, why wasn't the state of Nevada involved? If Jean Peters had really received a codicil from Howard Hughes—which was so ridiculous that he actually chuckled to himself on the cot—it was a state matter, not a federal matter. Hughes, in the state of Nevada, allegedly left money to a woman in Nevada. So the first stab should have been to follow the money trail—which did not exist—in Nevada. So where was the state of Nevada in this farce? Maybe the state of Nevada knew better.

Where was the FBI?

Who told the press about his arrest . . . er . . . *detention*?

What the hell was *really* going on?

CHAPTER 9

HOWARD HUGHES ARRIVES IN LAS VEGAS

There is an old Chinese curse: "May you live in interesting times." This, however, like many parables, is apocryphal. There is no such Chinese curse. The closest Chinese pronouncement is an expression from a 1627 short story from Feng Menglong's *Stories to Awaken the World*. It was blatantly plagiarized from Wikipedia, "宁為太平犬，莫做亂离人" (*nìng wéi tàipíng quǎn, mò zuò luàn lí rén*),and is usually translated as "Better to be a dog in a peaceful time than to be a man in a chaotic (warring) period."

Historically speaking, human history is roughly 5,000 years in length. That is, the written record goes back about 5,000 years. The first pharaoh was Menes, about 2925 BCE. He unified Upper and Lower Egypt into what Egyptologists call "The Old Kingdom." Students refer to it as "ancient Egypt" that thrived about the time their parents were born.

Humor aside, civilization as we know it, has been around for quite a while. A lot has happened in those 5,000 years as long as you are talking about the haves. For the have-nots, not so much. For the poor, Old Kingdom, New Kingdom, Assyrian, Babylonian, High Middle Ages,

Gilded Age, Western Frontier, Roaring Twenties, and the Computer Age are all the same. For them, their personal history is an agonizing scramble for survival. Cities, states, countries, and empires come and go, but the plight of the poor does not change. In this sense, Chinese history is no different than that of Western Civilization: the upper 3% (called the rich) control 70% of the money (called the economy), and the remaining 97% of the population (called the people) have to fight tooth and nail, timecard, and 401K to see how the other 30% of the money in the economy is divided.

Technology may not have brought a change to the percentages and dynamics of making money, but it has expanded the range of opportunity for 97% of the population to grow their wealth. This has been a gift that keeps on giving.

But the transition has not been without pain. The year 1848 was known as "The Year of Revolution" in Europe because the steam engine put hundreds of thousands of workers out of a job. A generation later, the steam engine had created ten times that many jobs worldwide. The newfangled steamships and railroads stimulated the infant steel and petroleum industries. Docks had to be built for the larger ships. Rail lines had to be constructed for the increased cargo and passenger traffic. Bridges had to leap rivers, and millions of square miles of fertile land could now be farmed because there was a rail transportation system to get corn, wheat, and rye from the few farmers who grew the harvest to the hundreds of people who would eat the crop. Hundreds of thousands of workers had to be hired to make the steam-powered ships and trains. Thousands of miles of track had to be laid, and every engine that used every mile of that track had to be watered, oiled, repaired, replaced, guarded, and upgraded.

The railroad also shortened the cattle drives. Before the railroad, the cattle had to be driven from Texas to Chicago. With a rail link in Abilene, cattle drives were shorter; thus, the cattle were fatter, which led to more profit for the cattle barons. Joseph McCoy, the original "Real McCoy," established Abilene as the cattle-exporting railhead, and by 1870 the trails from Texas were chocked with cattle heading to Kansas.

A year later the city was seeing as many as 5,000 cowboys paid off in *a single day*, which made the businesses of Abilene very happy to see so many dollars running through their cash registers. But it infuriated the so-called good citizens of Abilene because of the problems 5,000 cowboys a day created. Abilene went from a flyspeck of civilization to cattle-rush boomtown in less than a handful of years. It did not take long before the townsfolk grew very tired of the cowboys shooting up the town and the only marshal spending all his time living the highlife in the Alamo Saloon and sporting ladies of the evening on his arm. That marshal was James B. "Wild Bill" Hickok. There was not a dry eye uptown when, in 1871, Hickok was fired and the railheads for cattle moved to Wichita, Ellsworth, and Newton. During the heyday of Abilene, about four years, more than three million cattle made it to market.

None of these technological changes came to America overnight, but they did come. They also came with a price. Technology moved forward like a juggernaut and crushed all in its path. Technological advance is neither good nor bad; it is like mathematics. Numbers are neither good nor bad. They are simply a way to chart progress. Technology will advance a civilization, but it comes with a rather ugly underbelly. In the prop wash of advancing technology is the human garbage who find it easier to steal a dollar rather than earn an honest dollar. It would be comforting to say that "what goes around comes around," and those who lie, cheat, and steal eventually "get what's coming to them." In many cases they do. But enough do not end up paying some price, that the expression "crime does not pay" is inaccurate. A better expression is that "crime does not pay if you are stupid." The smartest criminals are lawyers.

Bullet arrived in Las Vegas at the most opportune time for a young man who was both honest and prescient. As to the first, "honest" is a term that has two meanings. Actions that are honest in one locale could be illegal in another. In Nevada, prostitution is legal, while across its borders in all directions, it is illegal. In some states, recreational marijuana is legal, while in Nevada it was not. Gambling is legal but regulated in Nevada. Gambling is illegal in many states—but many of these same states allow games of chance that are not considered "gambling," such as lotteries, Bingo, pull tabs, Internet poker, and fantasy sports "games of skill" and have two blind eyes for high stakes card games in private homes.

Bullet was honest in the old-fashioned sense of the term. Though not a religious man by any stretch of the definition, he had absorbed the basic lesson of all religions; in that, you make your own life enjoyable or excruciating on the basis of the cycles you generate. Evil and poor lifestyle decisions catch up to you fairly quickly. Being good does not necessarily or immediately win you any earthly delights, but it does allow you to sleep soundly and not worry about the tax man, mob collectors, or the ghost of your Baptist grandmother.

Bullet was also prescient because he could see the shadows of the future of Las Vegas starting to fall when he arrived in the summer of 1971. The city was in the midst of a deluge of money from the Teamster Pension Funds, and the mob ran the city as if they were potentates of a Calafat. The Strip was their Canaan, their Land of Milk and Honey, and as long as they continued to dance the bunny hug with the Teamsters, nothing was going to change. The mob controlled the Nevada legislature, and the Teamsters were dropping tens of millions of dollars a year into the casinos on a hope and a prayer that the investment would pay off before too many truck drivers retired. It seemed there was no power on heaven or earth that could stop the mob/teamster steamroller.

But there was a fatal flaw in the apparent strength of the coalition: Las Vegas was catering to a low-bar clientele. By offering almost-free rooms and complimentary drinks to get gamblers into the casinos, the casinos were primarily attracting cheapskate tourists and low-dollar gamblers. The shows did well, but, in the 1970s, Las Vegas was not even a shadow of what it would be in a decade. The big problem was that the mob and the Teamsters were so focused on the nickels and dimes that *they could see* rather than the Benjamins they *could not.*

They were in for a surprise.

The Strip got a well-needed public face-lift starting in 1966 when Howard Hughes came to town. He was different because he came with gob loads of cash, a Niagara Falls of lucre into the paltry creek that Las Vegas was. He came with cash in amounts so large that it staggered the imagination of even the most jaded of casino owners. Fresh from the sale of his Trans World Airlines for $566 million, Hughes had money to burn. Burn it he did. In rapid succession, he made cash purchases of the Sands, Landmark, Silver Slipper, Castaways, and Frontier. He moved so fast and snatched up so many casinos that there was palpable fear in Carson City that he would monopolize the Strip. So the state government stepped in and stopped Hughes's rapacious buying.

But Hughes was not through. He not only upgraded his casinos but also brought in his own business-management style. In the bad old days, the belief was "it took a gambler to run a gambling joint." The mob had used this excuse to move its people into casino management. Now the mob was in for a surprise. Hughes did not believe in that maxim. He removed the old hands—for *old hands* read *mob-connected*—and replaced them with business people, many of them Mormons with unwavering moral compasses, who had cold water in their veins. He raised the price of his rooms, which brought in a higher-class clientele, and chased organized crime—the organization and the criminals—out of Las Vegas. As they left, so did the taint of organized crime. This encouraged the larger national hospitality chains to move in, and Las Vegas doubled the number of travelers per year within the decade. They stayed in rooms that were not complementary and paid full price for meals and drinks.

It was midway through this period of transition that Bullet arrived in Las Vegas. It did not take him long to understand the big picture. Rather, what was happening was so clear that even the card dealers who lived uptown knew that change was in the sirocco. While the mob was still running large swaths of the Strip, their days were numbered.

But the mob wasn't going very fast. Tony "the Ant" Spilotro was still a power in town. Everyone knew he had murdered Leo Foreman—not that any of the card dealers cared. Spilotro and Foreman were way above their pay grade. When Spilotro and Bompensiero bumped off Tamara Rand in 1975, the feeling was pretty much the same. Bompensiero was a lot worse than Spilotro. It was said of him that he "had buried more bones than could be found in the brontosaurus room of the Museum of Natural History."

The moment Spilotro was squeezed out of the casinos in 1979 and started fencing stolen goods at the Gold Rush, Ltd., everyone knew he was finished. Everyone, that is, except Tony the Ant. It was going to be a while before Spilotro finally ended up beaten and buried alive in Enos, Indiana—as far away from Las Vegas as the mob could lure him—but when Bullet came to Las Vegas, everyone knew that Tony the Ant was a dead man walking.

So was the mob.

It was still going to take a while for the forces of righteousness to supplant the dark side, but victory was coming. From the card dealers up, everyone knew you had to choose one side or the other. There was a great amount of money to be made with the mob, but you had to take that money and run. On the other hand, if you expected to live long and were willing to make your money legally and over the long run, you sided with Howard Hughes, Harry Reid, and the Nevada Gaming Control Board. Bullet knew on which side of the bread was the butter.

Even more important, he knew which card dealers had been on the dark side. They may have ended up with Bullet after the mob left town, but they were dangerously and surreptitiously maintaining their connections in Chicago, New Jersey, and Orlando. Organizations like the mob do not go quietly. Or disappear. They just go dark. There was too much money running around in Las Vegas for the forces of greed to surrender. They simply moved away in name and became more sophisticated and harder to spot.

Even more important, as the times changed, so did the rules. The grab-and-dash days of the old Las Vegas were gone, but there were still remnants of the mob in town. They were not in the casinos, but they were not out of gambling. Everyone knew who they were, of course, and for the most part left them alone. The old mobsters were retired and would occasionally get together in a coffee shop or Waffle House because they were not allowed in so much as the parking lot of any of the casinos. There were no young bucks earning their bones on the street, but it was an open secret that some casinos washed money. You could take the mob out of Las Vegas, but you could not take Las Vegas out of the mob. But, by and large, the mob was gone. Most important, as far as Bullet was concerned, they were gone. He had not dealt with them when they were in Las Vegas, and he didn't deal with their moles after the mob was more or less gone.

The upside of getting the mob out of Las Vegas was that tourism took a jump in both number and quality. What had been a good day in 1972 was a low day in 1982. There were no empty hotel rooms. It was boom time at the tables. Depression, recession, stagflation, or inflation, Las Vegas was packed. It defied the economic models. The Law of Supply and Demand was violated every day on the Strip. The more casinos and hotels there were, the more tourists arrived. The Law of Decreasing Marginal Utility had no relevance, and the concept of elasticity was turned on its head while, at the same time, there was perfect competition on the Strip. People just kept coming.

For Bullet, there was no magic on the Strip. It was where he worked. The years may have been good for Las Vegas, but they were not particularly fruitful for those who worked in the casinos. The hours were long and the pay not particularly good. There was no glamor in the pits, and unless you could move up to the games with the high rollers, tips were miniscule compared to the winnings at the table. By the winnings, this meant the take of the house. Bullet saw the house making millions, and his salary stayed uncomfortably close to minimum wage. Tips were welcome, and as long as he did not report them, he could save for a rainy day.

Even without a college degree, he slipped into the upper crust of the working class, and there he stayed. As men and women with college degrees but with less talent and lower IQs moved up the casino food chain, Bullet remained a worker bee. He did pick up some units at the local junior college but found the classes boring. The very classes that should have been a cornucopia of worldly relevance—specifically economics and business—were misplaced in Las Vegas. He came away with an AA, which helped his career as much as a certificate from AA.

But he was not a dolt.

He could see where the money was; he just could not reach there. So he continued working for the casino and slowly moved up in the ranks. He was moved off the tables and then out of the pits. For a while he was in the counting room. This increased his base pay but denied him tips, so he was basically running in place. He was a dray animal, not a thoroughbred, and until that changed, he would finish his life no better off than a janitor or clothing salesman.

One of the saving graces in his life was that he was asexual. That is to say, he was neither gay nor straight. He had his proclivities but found that paying for them was better—and cheaper—than being married. He had nothing against marriage; he just didn't believe it was for him. But that was his only saving grace. He could not look upon life as a grand adventure because he was on a treadmill to nowhere. He was caught in the continuum of work-pension-die, none of the three being rewarding. It was not so much that he thought he deserved more; it was that he understood he was going somewhere. Where, he did not know. Just that he did not truly believe he would end up retired, living in some remote corner of a trailer park in Las Vegas. The same could not be said of the men and women with whom he worked. From his point of view, they were going nowhere. He, on the other hand, was going somewhere. Where, he did not know. But he knew that when that *somewhere* crested the horizon, he would know where to go. As he could not see his destination, he could not move in that direction.

Yet.

It was the *yet* that made him different from everyone else in the casino. He had a destiny to be fulfilled, and it was not work-pension-die. He knew he was going somewhere. It was just a matter of time and circumstance before he would figure out what it was. He was going to get a shot at the big time—at least one, anyway. It was the reality of life. He just had to be patient and prepared for that one time when he could grab for the brass ring. Fortune favors the audacious, but by 1990 Bullet was not so sure there was a brass ring left for him to grab.

CHAPTER 10

HARRY KELLY, AUDITOR FOR THE STATE OF NEVADA

There are only two jokes about auditors; the rest are true stories. Auditors are the wallflowers of business and make accountants appear to have a personality. A person becomes an auditor when he or she realizes he or she does not have the charisma to be an undertaker.

But not all auditors are stupid.

Harry Kelly was an auditor, and he was not stupid. He knew he was in a business that was more political than actuarial. If this were the case in Denver, Tallahassee, or Grand Rapids, he did not know. What he did know was that in Las Vegas, there were always powerful winds blowing in all directions. It really did not matter what the auditors found on the ground; everything went up the administrative chain of command. Unless a transgression discovered made it into the newspaper, he never knew if the malfeasance he and his team had uncovered made any difference. All he knew was that he would not see the same financial malfeasance the next year he and the team audited the same bank. This could mean that the bank had been reprimanded or, more likely, the bank altered its accounting procedures to hide what had been discovered the previous audit season.

He was also psychic.

He could see the future.

The moment he got the notice that he and his team were going to be pulled off their yearly March audit of Rutherford Bank and Trust to chase after some fantasy of $50 million from some Howard Hughes codicil laundering through casinos and banks that no longer existed, he knew he was being snookered.

Who was doing it and why, he had no idea.

But he didn't care.

It was just another political wind. He and his team would just have to tack to an oblique angle. They'd audit the Rutherford Bank and Trust later.

If not later, then the proceeding March.

After all, what could possibly go wrong between now and then?

CHAPTER 11

ZAPATA FINDS A NEW PROFESSION

If there was any one thing Zapata could say about life, it was that it was constantly taking her by surprise. At no time in her life could she say that she was living anything close to whatever the rest of the world called normal. There was no "same old, same old." There was no "for better or worse," from "pillar to post," "over hill and dale," or any other expression for life in the expected lane. She never knew from year to year what the future was going to offer—or force her to accept. Her life did not have incandescent moments, only the slow burn of embers.

This is not to say that she was being swept forward in life on the turbulent surface of a shoal-dotted river on which she was clinging to a broken spar for survival. That was a very poor metaphor to describe her years in Las Vegas. Her life could not be characterized or compartmentalized into anything approaching normal, even for the era and city in which she was living. She had started her adult life on the street as a throwaway teenager and clawed her way up as a card dealer, show girl, call girl, and Realtor. She had been a faux wife for several years for several men, of whom only one was not married. The relationships all started well and ended badly. But that was the price of her lifestyle. She knew it, accepted it, and moved through relationships as if they were doorways along a hotel corridor. She was out one door and into another with very little time in-between. She never knew what life-changing event was coming her way, only that it would arrive from an obtuse angle.

It could truly be said she started from the bottom. Within 18 months of her high school graduation, she had gone from being a pampered child of a successful real-estate family to a street person. In less than a year, she had lost her mother to lung cancer, her father to alcohol, and her stepmother to a fast-talking Charlie from some city on the East Coast that started with a B. The family real-estate business went down the maw of a Las Vegas real-estate whirlpool recession so fast that it didn't even leave flotsam.

Las Vegas, from the outside looking in, is a city of glamour, intrigue, and buildings so burgeoning in wealth that it leaks onto the streets in streams of chips and rivers of Benjis. On the inside, there was no looking out. It was a gritty town where the casinos paid minimum wage with the excuse that tips would move their workers into the working class. There may have been a lot of money *in* the casinos, *going into* the casinos and *transferring* from the casinos to the banks, but that money was eyeballed by an alphabet soup of state and federal regulators, along with casino accountants and shareholders. Trying to rob a casino was a fool's errand. There were a lot of nickel-and-dime scams and schemes, but by and large they were not even a drop in the bucket of casino profit. The only *big* robberies of casinos were Oceans 11, Oceans 12, and Oceans 13. The consistent big money on the outside was being made by trick-rolling or unlicensed bookies. Entrepreneurially speaking, Las Vegas was a Republican's worst nightmare because, here, regulation *increased* the profits of the private sector rather than acting as a stumbling block.

For Zapata, Las Vegas was a living horror story. She was broke and on the streets at a time when it was the only town in America that could have cared less about street people. They were invisible. The casinos and hotels of the Strip did not want them seen. When they meandered onto the Strip, they were escorted a few blocks away and told not to return. There were no shelters in those days, and the churches were distant in both miles and compassion. If you had the habit, you died with it.

Zapata's saving grace was that she was young and strong. She understood that she had to make her own way in the world and was willing to work rather than take handouts. She got a good job as a maid for the simple reason that she was white. Caucasian maids were a rarity in those days and were showcased by the services. These were service personnel who could be *seen* at parties rather than the usual invisible brown-and-black waiters who bussed tables and kept the flutes on the champagne tables full. For Zapata, the money was good because she was young and had no concept of saving for retirement. She could also live meanly and did not mind rooming with other maids. But after two years of being a showcase and making no more than she had her first day on the job, she transitioned to being a card dealer because they made tips. This was a step up financially but not mentally. Dealing cards was mind-numbing because you were not expected to be anything but an automaton. Card dealers treated everyone the same: winners, losers, whiners, deadbeats. They came and sat at your table, and you treated them all the same.

Two years later she was bored with cards.

It was still a man's world in the 1960s, and there was no *up* in the up-or-out world of Las Vegas. Even with a college degree, she would have found the ceiling to be of tinted Plexiglas. She spent a year in junior college before she ran out of money. Then it was back to dealing cards.

Two years thereafter, she was back to square one. She did not want to go back to being a maid, could not stomach another round of meaningless classes at junior college, and needed to get out of the pit before she went crazy. Financially she was no better off than she had been half a decade earlier, and now, for the first time in her life, she began to look forward to her old age rather than the next weekend.

What was particularly frightening to her was that she was working with women twice her age who were making exactly the same wages and tips she was. In them she saw her future. The only difference was that the other women had been through two, three, and some four marriages.

Or men. The two were not mutually exclusive. Yet here they were, still dealing cards in their fifties. What was going to happen to them in five years? What was going to happen to her in 20 years? Would she end up just like them?

Five years and one marriage later, she was, once again, back to where she started: dealing cards. But now she was pushing 30, and the clock was still ticking.

Life had a tendency to throw her curve balls. Just when she was expecting another speedball or slider, in came a pitch that clipped the far side of the box. Or maybe she knew it was in her cards. Either way, she was sitting on a barstool, which, for her, was rare, as she was not a drinker—or, for that matter, a drug person. In both cases, she had seen what the demon rum and blow could do. So she did not indulge. Or experiment. She was happy to be stone-cold sober and straight at parties where everyone else was howling at the moon or kicking the gong around. It was thus odd that she should be sitting on a barstool in a casino—of all places—and lamenting how rotten life was in general and how hers was in the sewer at that moment. Looking back, of course, she understood what she did next was par for the course in Las Vegas. The bartender told her she was still young and good looking, so she should try hooking.

At the very least, it paid.

Very well.

Very well.

He told her to get dressed provocatively and come back to the bar, and he would see what he could do for her. She didn't have much of a choice. She was running out of money and options. So she went back to her shared bedroom, dressed up, and went down to the bar.

It was the worst night of her life.

But it was profitable.

Too profitable to give up.

She kept up the act, and the money rolled in, sometimes as much as $1,000 a night. She had never seen money like that! She dressed uptown, got a hot car, and started to drink because she needed it now. It was dirty work. It was demeaning work. But it paid very, very well.

71

Too good to give up.

She was making so much money that she forgot to save any. There was no Plexiglas ceiling in this profession. Life was good. Then, once again, life threw her a curve—two of them, actually. Later in life she would call them "wake-up calls." As in all wake-up calls, the twin forces—independently and combined—blasted through the six inches of cranial bone she had built around her ego and spoke to her with a force as if it was the voice of God. The twin forces were Sandoval "Bullet" Wisnoski and Myrrh Frankincense. The message was right out of a book she had rejected as a card dealer—John 8:11: "Go now and leave your life of sin."

CHAPTER 12

THE IRS TAKES THE BAIT

No one in the bowels of the office of the IRS in Las Vegas actually believed the copy of the codicil was authentic. Even if it was, that $50 million was l-o-n-g g-o-n-e. There was not a shred of evidence that this codicil was legitimate and a mountain of logic that it was the stuff of conspiracy buffs. It was bogus. One of the agents even called it an outhouse financial fantasy.

But the newspapers and television stations were clamoring for a statement.

Not only that, the *Las Vegas Scandal, Inc.* had already quoted a senior IRS official who had allegedly stated that the IRS was looking into the codicil. The IRS was going to have to do something.

So someone upstairs said, "Take a stab at it."

So someone in the trenches had to.

That someone did some digging and came up with a probate record from six months earlier. A Jean Peters of Las Vegas had named a Harold Charles Dobbins as her sole heir. This included all her property, including her business, the Peters Title Company of Las Vegas, and "all assets, documents, and contents of her safety deposit box."

73

There were three Jean Peters in the Las Vegas phone book. Two had absolutely no idea what the IRS was talking about. The third had left a message on her answering machine that she was "out of the country on a medical emergency."

Harold Charles Dobbins was easier to find. He had been a casino accountant for the Cypress Casino. The IRS agent made a call to the Nevada Gaming Control Board and found that the Cypress had been subject to more than a few investigations regarding the laundering of money along with close, possibly and probably inappropriate, associations between casino management and out-of-state gambling interests. There was nothing solid here, but then, again, Harold Charles Dobbins had been an accountant at one casino for more than four decades, and if there was any one place in Las Vegas where $50 million in cash could disappear, it would be a casino.

Maybe a talk with this Harold Charles Robbins was in order.

But by then it was Friday afternoon.

Late Friday afternoon.

CHAPTER 13

PROF AND THE CODICIL

Prof loved it when he could use the day's newspaper in his classroom. It was a constant reminder to his students that there was no such thing as the present. That illusionary locale was simply the razor's edge where the past meets the future. This semester he was blessed because of the sudden appearance of the Hughes codicil in every newspaper in town.

For his Tuesday class, he brought in two dozen copies of the morning papers and passed them around. They were loaded with photographs of Howard Hughes, Jean Peters, Bette Davis, Ava Gardner, and the H-1 Racer. The papers were crammed with stories of Howard Hughes, his life as an aviator, his loves, and his descent into insanity that was being called *eccentricities* because only the poor are *crazy*.

Front and center in all the newspapers were sidewalk shots of Harold Dobbins as he was zipping into the underground garage beneath the Las Vegas Police Station. There were sidebars on Harold Charles Dobbins as to who he was and why he was not under arrest but being held as a material witness. There was not a lot of information on Dobbins. This was not because he was an elusive character like a figure keeping a low profile but as though he were a low-level civil servant whose name only

75

appeared on the list of public employees. There was a single head shot of Dobbins from his high school yearbook, and he looked just as goofy as everyone else does in those kinds of pictures.

Prof loved the incident because it gave him yet another chance to pull the past into the future. The explanation of a codicil was easy. It was a piece of paper, part of a collection of papers. In this case, that collection of papers was called a will. Usually, he told his class, a will is a document that outlines who gets what if and when the person signing the will dies. In this case, it was critical to find the will of Howard Hughes—the actual will of the deceased, not this codicil—because there were three important items to be considered. First was some boilerplate wording that all wills contain. The specific boilerplate was the line, usually in the first paragraph, which states that this will negates all previous wills that may exist. This is an important line because it makes it legally certain that this will is the real McCoy and all others may have been the real McCoy when they were signed, but if those wills were dated *before* this last will, they were null and void. The second critical feature of the will is when it was written and, third, that it was properly signed.

However—and this was a very important *however*—this particular case added a new dimension to the Hughes's will conspiracy. First, a codicil is not a will. What this means is that it is not subject to the boilerplate sentence. A good example, Prof said, would be a father selling his automobile a week before he died. He sold the car for $4,500, he and the buyer signed a bill of sale, and then the father cashed the check. Once the father cashed the check, the car belonged to the new buyer even if the new buyer had not yet registered the change of name on the title of the automobile with the State of Nevada Department of Motor Vehicles. Then, since the father had died unexpectedly, his will could not have been changed regarding the automobile. So if the will reads that the automobile that has just been sold goes to his son George, George does not get the car because his father no longer owned it. That makes the reference to the car in the will meaningless.

In the case of the Hughes codicil, as Prof told the class, the date of the codicil had absolutely no importance at all. If the codicil was authentic—and for the purposes of academic discussion, he asked the class to accept that possibility—it made no difference when it was signed. That is, as long as it was signed before Howard Hughes died. As long as the codicil was signed by Howard Hughes before April 5, 1976, the day he died in Houston, Texas, it was a legitimate transfer of property even if that specific $50 million was mentioned in a later Howard Hughes will.

"Here is how a will is probated," Prof told the class. "A person makes a will. He names someone to probate the will, possibly the family lawyer. To probate a will means to dispense the assets of the deceased the way the deceased wanted the assets spread around. The person dies. The family lawyer opens the will and tells everyone assembled who gets what. End of story."

But in this case, the person was Howard Hughes. The good news was that he was worth about $4 billion in today's dollars, Prof noted. But bad news came in threes. First, Hughes did not have an immediate family. Second, he had no children or grandchildren. Third, he left no will.

So who was going to get that money?

That was such a good question no one had an answer for.

Everyone remotely related to Howard Hughes, the Howard Hughes Medical Institute, ex-wives, illegitimate children, people claiming to be illegitimate children, fakes, frauds, and scam artists, descended on the fortune like magpies on a gut pile. Some of the speculative claims included the possibility of a love child with Amelia Earhart—who never had any children—and a number of black claimants even though Hughes had been a notorious racist. One of the more bizarre claimants was actress Terry Moore, who claimed she had been secretly married to Howard Hughes—twice! While it was true she lived with Hughes briefly in the 1940s, she could not produce a certificate from either marriage and had not mentioned to Hughes the three alleged marriages to the three men she married *after* she had supposedly been married— and never divorced—to Hughes twice!

The most widely publicized scam was perpetrated by a gas-station attendant by the name of Melvin Earle Dummar. Dummar claimed he had picked up Hughes hitchhiking in the desert. (A man worth billions, who owned a substantial chunk of Las Vegas, hitchhiking in the desert?) Supposedly, Hughes had given Dummar a codicil, giving Dummar 1/16 of the Hughes estate. The court did not believe the Dummar codicil and declined to give him any money.

At the end of the day, a collection of about 200 legitimate, distant relatives split $1.5 billion, and the rest went to the Hughes Medical Clinic.

Linking the Hughes codicil to a real life, historical lesson, Prof noted, at the end of the day it did not matter whether the codicil was real or forged. For the purposes of his class, it also did not matter what happened to the money.

"Historically speaking," he told the class, "it is important to keep in mind that ownership is a very fluid concept. It is also an issue bedeviling us to this day. Quite a bit of land in the American West was originally Indian land. Even if the Kennewick Man proved to be a legitimate precursor to the American Indians, it made no difference. Land in North America that was not Canadian, state or federal allowed for squatter's rights. That means that if someone lived on land that was not Canadian, state, or federal acreage for seven years, it was theirs. The only proof of the existence of Kennewick Man was 8,500 years old, which was a lot longer than seven years. Even if there had been someone before the Indians, the Indians had squatter's rights to all of North America. Later, white settlers signed treaties and land agreements with American Indians—tribes and individuals—and these were legal documents. If those treaties were violated, as many of them were, could the Indians legitimately take the case to court? This is a good question, but no one has answered it yet.

"On a nuts-and-bolts basis," he said, "when linking the concept of ownership to real life, students should keep in mind that a sale does not necessarily mean that property has been transferred. Just because you sell something does not mean you can wash your hands of the property. If a store sells you meat that is bad, and you get sick, you can sue the store even though you paid for the meat and left the store. If you sell a car and do not tell the buyer the transmission is going bad, the man who bought the car can get his money back."

Prof wrapped up the day's lecture by stating he had absolutely no idea why the IRS was scrambling to find the codicil. Even if it turned out to be authentic, it was a moot point. Even if there had been $50 million, the money had changed hands long ago. Even if the money had been stolen, the statute of limitations had long since run out. It would be like your grandfather finding a bag of money and investing it half a century ago. Even if he stole the original money, what is left is still your money.

Further, even if it were true that the original $50 million had been stolen and the IRS could prove it, Dobbins did not own it. Jean Peters did. According to the newspaper, Jean Peters was still alive and in Manilla. Since the newspaper reporters had uncovered the fact that Jean Peters had breast cancer, it was logically assumed that she was in the Philippines as a medical tourist, someone who goes to a foreign country for a medical procedure. Surgery is cheaper in the Philippines than the United States. Until Jean Peters died, the $50 million was still her money regardless of what investments were made by Harold Dobbins in her name—if he made any at all. If she died, and the investments were transferred to Harold Charles Dobbins, he could not transfer the investment from her name to his name without the money coming to the attention of the IRS as an inheritance.

"So," Prof finished, "what was going here? What was the backstory?"

CHAPTER 14

THE MORPHEAN UNIVERSE

There is an old musician's joke that starts with a jazz great dying and going to heaven. He is met at the pearly gates by an old man who tells him he played so well on earth that he's going to be included in the Jazz All-Time Greats of the World. He's going to spend eternity playing alongside the best—men like Sachmo, Ellington, Davis, Basie, Armstrong, and Joplin. "You'll fit right," the old man tells him. "As a matter of fact, your first concert is in a few hours. But there's only one problem. God's got this girlfriend who is a singer . . ."

The human mind, Eastern and Western, primordial and modern, primitive and advanced, has always had a difficult time grappling with the non-tactile. In the tactile world, we believe that if we can touch an object, it exists. An apple exists because we can touch it. Complicating the picture, we can also believe in things that we can see but do not exist. A rainbow is a good example. It exists in our visual perception, but it is an illusion created by the prism effect of light passing through water in the atmosphere in liquid form. The prism effect of light on water in its solid state in the atmosphere is called a sundog. But neither the rainbow nor the sundog can be touched. They do not exist. But they can be seen.

The non-tactile is substantially more complicated. The Greeks tried to simplify the philosophical complexity by dividing the world into the physical and spiritual, but this led to more problems than it solved. The failure to divide the spirit world into more compartments—to use a tactile definition for a non-tactile world—implies that your great-grandmother is, at this very moment, dancing with unicorns and leprechauns. Organized religion did not clear up the matter. While the three great religions of the world—Judaism, Christianity, and Islam—all worship the same supreme deity and have a day of judgment, none of these religions give any indication as to what happens between the time an individual dies and when the day of judgment arrives. Thus, there is the very real—or unreal—possibility that Mohammad, Jesus, Hitler, Mozart, and Bruce Lee are cavorting together, waiting for that great moment of division, with the good going one way and the evil another.

Further, all of mankind, from the cave to the computer age in all cultures, know that there is some manner of crossover from the non-tactile world. While only a few people have seen a ghost or voyager from another dimension, almost all humans have had a brush with the supernatural. It could have been the feeling of a presence of an old friend who had passed, the flick of a shape going upstairs in the manner of a long-dead dog, a grandparent speaking to you in your dreams, or even the aligning of temporal events at critical moments that leads religious people to assert that "God works in mysterious ways."

While we accept the reality of different dimensions of the spiritual world, we have no problem living with the different dimensions of the tactile world. Even though we encounter those dimension on a daily basis, it does not faze us that we are dealing with imaginary objects in a brick-and-mortar world. An excellent example is money.

Suppose you are in a classroom with 50 people. If you were to ask all 50 people to put every penny of money they had in their pockets, wallets, and purses on a table in the center of the room, how much money do you think would be there? Considering the average student has about $5 in cash on their person at any one time, the total cash on the table will be $250. But if the students were asked to guess at the *accumulated* money in their collective checking and savings accounts, the total could reasonably be $50,000. If the students were asked to write down their net worth, the number would be five times that great.

With the exception of the $250 on the table in the center of the room, all the other dollar figures are imaginary. If student Julie Jones went to her bank and asked to see the $1,000 she had in her checking account, the bank official would laugh and say that her $1,000 "did not exist." It was just ink on paper on her monthly statement. At the bank it was just an electronic file—made up of electrons that did exist but a "file" that did not.

Even though that $1,000 "did not exist," Julie Jones can use a plastic card at the grocery store and get tactile objects like soup, ice cream, peanut butter, and coffee using imaginary, non-tactile objects called numbers from a checking account that has her personal money that "does not exist." Most important, no one in this financial transactional chain has any doubts that the alleged-to-be-money "is real."

Moving one step back from the nickel-and-dime transactions, the tactile world becomes Morphean. The term is from the Greek god of dreams, who watches over people while they sleep, shapes their dreams, and can metamorphosize in human form. Banks, the brick-and-mortar building where we keep our checking and saving accounts, exist in a Morphean world. They do not deal in cash; they deal in provenance. A provenance in the art world is a chronological history of the ownership of a piece of art. If someone inherited a Picasso and wanted to sell the painting, the art dealer would require the provenance. This piece of paper would indicate who originally bought the painting from Picasso, on what date it was purchased, and how much was paid. Each subsequent sale would be recorded on the provenance chronologically to the current seller. The provenance, like the title of a car, gives a history of its owners.

When it comes to money in a bank—which does not exist—the bank requires proof of ownership, its provenance. If someone deposits a check for $1 million from British Petroleum in their checking account, the bank would check the provenance of the $1 million before it allowed one dime of the $1 million to be withdrawn. Even though what British

Petroleum gave the bank was not cash, it was treated as cash. This is a fairly simple explanation of money in the private sector, but when it comes to the public sector, the Morphean realities—which do not exist—become far more complicated.

Then there is the *big* money in banks: mortgages.

Keeping the mortgage convolutions as simple as possible, when a couple wants to borrow $500,000 for a home, they apply to a local bank for the money. The couple fills out paperwork and submits it to the home-loan department in the local bank. If the couple's credit is good, and they have the necessary down payment, the local bank submits the paperwork to a larger bank that bundles it with hundreds of other loan-application requests and submits that bundle to a mega-bank that borrows the money from the federal government from Fannie Mae or Freddie Mac. When the federal money is lent to the mega-bank, the mega-bank adds a modest percentage as a transaction fee and loans it to the bank which provided it the loan that, in turn, adds a modest percentage as a transaction fee and then lends it to the local bank, which adds a modest percentage as a transaction fee, and then gives the home loan to the couple. Thus, the couple is, in essence, borrowing their own money and paying three banks for the privilege.

Enter the Morphean world. The federal government requires that the money it is *lending* for mortgages be *used* for mortgages. This is a fine requirement that has no basis in reality because federal money is indistinguishable from private-sector money. Once that mega-bank receives the money, it is the mega-bank's money. It *was* federal money, and *now it is* private-sector money.

In reality—an odd term to use in a Morphean universe—the mega-bank is not borrowing mortgage money for mortgages. It is borrowing massive amounts of mortgage moneys for smaller banks who *assert* they will use that money for mortgages. If a smaller bank uses the mortgage money for car loans, the mega-bank is not on the hook, because it is only acting as a pass-through of mortgage money, not a mortgage lender.

Now the Morphean world gets more complicated. When $500,000— which does not exist as cash—is in the bank account of Freddie Mac, it is federal money. The moment the $500,000 transfers from Freddie Mac to the mega-bank, it is no longer federal money. It is private-sector money. The only link is a piece of paper—or, most likely, an electronic file—that indicates money in a certain amount that does not exist has been transferred to the mega-bank for mortgages. The money that does not exist is then washed through larger banks to the small bank where a family filed the original paperwork for the loan.

But this makes the transaction seem simple and straightforward when it is nothing but. The loan dollars that the couple is agreeing to pay back over the 30-year life of the loan is not the small bank's money. It is still federal money that has passed through the coffers of the larger bank and the mega-bank. It has also been washed in the sense that the original money (that never existed) from the federal government has been mixed with private-sector money (which also does not exist) in the coffers of the mega-bank, larger bank, and small bank.

Only the provenance remains.

So if the loan goes bad, the institution holding the title to the home is the one stuck with the loss. If the couple who applied for the original loan defaults, the small local bank is only out the monthly servicing fee. It is some other bank up the financial food chain all the way to Fannie Mae and Freddie Mac that is stuck with the loss. This leaves the local bank in the fiscal clear. It has lost nothing but a small, monthly servicing fee. Even better, or worse depending whether you are the bank or the public, if the small bank gets stuck with the home in default, the loan becomes one of bad debt. Bad debt is a write-off against taxes. Even more delicious, the bank can write off the default as a bad debt, yet still own the home. Who knows, in five years that home worth $1 today because the economy is bad could be worth $500,000 again when the local economy turns around.

Over the years, Bullet and Jigger continued to meet at the crossroads where imaginary money became real and real money became imaginary. Casino money in cash came into Rutherford Bank and Trust, where it was transformed into an electronic file. Then the real money was sent on to the Federal Depository in San Francisco, where it was also transformed into an electronic file, this time in the name of the Rutherford Bank and Trust. When the Triple Pines needed cash, the process was reversed. Rutherford Bank and Trust then traded electrons for real cash at the Federal Depository in San Francisco. The cash—which did exist—was transported to Las Vegas by an armored car to Rutherford Bank and Trust, where it was traded to the Triple Pines as money that did exist for an adjustment to the casino's electronic file at the bank. It was electrons to cash and then cash to electrons, with the bank taking a slice of the trade of money that did exist to be put into Morphean files.

In terms of money that did exist, the Nevada Gaming Commission required a cash backup, dollar-for-dollar, for every chip on the floor. Even though the Triple Pines was a small casino, this meant about $30 million in cash during the week and twice that on weekends and holidays. Since there was short-term money to be made on interest, Bullet made his cash deposits to banks on Mondays and Tuesdays. Then he would take cash out on Fridays for the weekend. Millions of dollars were going into and out of the Rutherford Bank and Trust every week. It got even more hectic during the holidays and over the Christmas week when the Triple Pines could need as much as $100 million. All in cash.

Even with this contact between the two men, they were not close. It was not that they disliked each other. It was that "like" was not in either man's vocabulary. One did not "like" someone in the casino or banking business. Liking someone usually led to lending money or finding oneself drawn into a scheme to skim a few dollars here and there. So neither man "liked" anyone. They both had many acquaintances but no friends.

The one thing that Jigger had in Bullet's eyes was longevity. Bullet had been crossing paths with Jigger for a decade under circumstances that gave each credibility to the other. Jigger had been a bartender who did not drink. Bullet patronized bars as places for quiet business conversations, but he did not drink. For both men, a saloon was a place to do business, and drinking did not lead to good business decisions. Jigger had been eighty-sixing drunks for thirty years and knew the price of alcoholism. All of Bullet's business meetings for the Triple Pines Casino were off-site.

This is not to say that there was anything illegal or unsavory going on. But it is to say that the minions of casino regulation had eyes and ears everywhere. They were rumored to regularly tap phones and intercept e-mails. They did conduct snap audits and occasionally spent phony Benjamins to make sure the casino staff knew the difference between a bogus bill and the Real McCoy. Bullet liked the Bullion Lounge because he had been going there for ten years, and Jigger never once gave any indication he had ever seen Bullet before.

Even more important, both men habituated the same specialty brothel in Las Vegas. Prostitution was legal in Nevada, and visiting a brothel was not unusual for a resident of Las Vegas. That being said, the services of the brothels that advertised remained within a standard deviation of the mean. To go beyond that fuzzy line required a connection that few tourists had. As a result, these establishments had regular clients from the Strip and the city. The services were exploitive, erotic, and expensive. Once again, Jigger and Bullet crossed paths but were like Baptists in a liquor store.

The first time the two actually had a real-world conversation was on the first day of Jigger's new job as the manager of Casino Transactions at Rutherford Bank and Trust. For the first time in their twin lives, there was an actual trading of information. Both were leery of the other, not only because of their past acquaintances but also because of the natural wariness between banker and casino minion in Las Vegas, a testiness because of the ongoing cross-hairing by regulators. While the Nevada Gaming Control Board did not audit bank records, the SEC did. But there was no regulatory wall between the two agencies and each looked over the other's records with agonizing regulatory.

Further, the casinos and banks in Las Vegas had a unique problem in the annals of business: they had too much money. Money as in cash. In the world of finance, cash *does* make enemies. In the case of the casinos, the Nevada Gaming Control Board, the Securities and Exchange Commission, the Internal Revenue Service, the Federal Bureau of Investigation, the State of Nevada, and the City of Las Vegas were absolutely, positively sure that the casinos and banks—individually, collectively, colluding, and in fast-forming-and-fast-dissipating company shells and cabals—were laundering cash. It was the general belief that moneys from illegal enterprises in Nevada and from across the United States were being funneled into and through Las Vegas casinos and banks. This doubled the headaches for the casinos and banks because it forced them to be doubly careful with both the books and actual collection, storage, and transfer of cash. From the casino floor to the accounting room through the armored-car services into and out of the bank vault and eventually to the Federal Reserve Bank in San Francisco, every slip of paper called cash was counted, double-counted, and triple-counted. Even then every federal and state agency believed that somehow the casinos, banks, or combined were somehow beating the system. It was an arrangement of ongoing suspicion.

More damaging, if there was as much as a hiccup of a problem, an audit was instantly ordered. This was both time-consuming and strained casino and bank personnel. For the state and federal regulators, this was their purpose in life. For the casinos and banks, it meant pulling people off their usual job and demanding that they explain a matter of dialectic hairsplitting through which no one made a dime. In cases like these—suspiciously far too frequent to be reasonable—the banks looked upon the casinos as the troublemakers, while the casinos returned the suspicion. It was never *our problem*, so why are you auditing *us*?

Thus, it was that there was a testy meeting of the two the first time they had to deal with each other on more than a casual professional basis. Both were well aware of the multitudinous sets of eyes watching their every move. Both were also aware that whatever they did would be double- and triple-checked back to the casino as well as from the bank to the Federal Reserve Bank in San Francisco.

For both men, their interactions were brief and professional. Jigger's connection with the casino was merely to log in the total numbers of boxes escorted into the bank by Bullet from the armored car. Jigger, Bullet, and the armored-car driver of the day—the last selected at random in upper levels of the armored-car company—would all sign a form in triplicate attesting to the delivery of the proper number of boxes.

Then each would get a copy of the form, and all would go their separate ways. Bullet would make a dozen such deliveries a week to a random selection of banks in Las Vegas. Jigger would authorize the transport of boxes of cash to the Federal Reserve Bank in San Francisco on a random basis as well. As long as the Federal Reserve counting of the money in San Francisco matched the same amount that left the casino—that had been counted by the casino accounting department and verified by the Nevada Gaming Control Board—all was, as was said on the street, "peachy keen."

The rest of Jigger's time was spent with real-estate transactions handled by the bank. It was in this capacity that he was uniquely qualified. In reality, the retired bankers who were teaching classes at the junior college were keeping an eye out for a certain type of individual. Having spent their lifetime in the arcane methods of banking, they knew that the big money was not in checking, savings, and loans; it was in mortgages. However—and this was a very large however—the fortunes were not being made with run-of-the-mill mortgage loans. These were, in actuality, only cover for where the real money was. "Buy land," Will Rogers had famously said. "They aren't making any more of it."

Las Vegas, like every other city in the United States, was involved with a cycle known locally humorously as the SSS, Triple S, or Trip for "triple." The last of these was sometimes replaced with "tripe" as a pun because, more often than not, that was what the bank was left with. The SSS stood for "Shell, Shuffle, and Shelf." It was a process triple-blessed by banks, because it was a way of washing property and decreasing taxable income. The SSS was a most excellent tax dodge as long as all the transactions were at arm's length. In other words, bank employees and/or board members could not profit *directly* from any sale of any property. They could—and did—profit but indirectly, at least one layer out from the actual transaction where money was exchanged for property.

As an example, making the process as simple as possible, the SSS process would start when a large non-Las Vegas corporation would decide it wanted to open an operation in Las Vegas. Suppose a large corporation wanted to build an upscale mall. To be profitable, the mall would have to be no smaller than 15 city blocks. Now the corporation has three options. It could find raw land, buy the acreage, and build the mall. The second option would be to buy out a dying mall and upgrade it. Or it could choose 15 city blocks where it wanted to put the mall and buy out every property owner within those city blocks. The last is by far the most expensive because it is not legal to use the power of eminent domain to move people who do not want to leave their neighborhood.

If the corporation decided on either of the first two options, the acquisition was a fairly simple transaction. The corporation could just buy the raw land or buy out of the old mall. Both of these actions are done every day in America. The third option is a bit trickier.

It is this third option that makes Las Vegas different from every other city in America. In most cities, malls chase neighborhoods. That is, as a city expands onto urban, suburban, and thereafter rural acreage, the mall corporations buy property *ahead* of the advance of civilization. Buying a dozen city blocks in a remote section of town where no one will live for five years is not unusual. Then, as the number of families per square acre goes up, the mall would begin to be built. As the number of families increase, the size of the mall expands financially correspondingly. By the time the rural landscape becomes tract housing, a critical population would have been reached, a full-sized mall would have been completed, and the stores therein would start making money hand over fist.

Las Vegas is different because the very big money is on the Strip, with less valuable property a block or two back.

But not further back than a block or two.

Thereafter, Las Vegas is just like every other city.

But the *big* money is on and near the Strip and no further back than a block or two. It is here that most of the SSS activity is concentrated.

As an example, if a luxury hotel wanted to expand into Las Vegas, it makes it known *very quietly* that it wants two city blocks no further back than one block back from the Strip. If the announcement is made loudly, there will be a mad scramble by banks and investment entrepreneurs to see if they can come up with two city blocks somewhere reasonably close to the Strip, but the price will be astronomical. (Now the Law of Supply and Demand works in Las Vegas.) Worse, if freelancers can lock up key pieces of property within those two blocks, they can pretty much demand what they want. Thus, the announcement is made quietly.

Suppose a luxury hotel makes such a *very quiet* announcement and states it has one zillion dollars at its disposal to buy two city blocks. Now the process of SSS begins. The individuals who have been informed that the hotel is looking at moving to Las Vegas must *very quietly* lock down the ownership of the specific lots where the hotel wants to relocate.

The first step is to form a shell corporation. The reason a shell corporation is formed is so that no one in Las Vegas knows until it is too late who is actually doing the buying. The shell is set up outside of Nevada, so the shell and its corporate officers cannot be found locally with a click of a mouse. Corporation records being public, anyone can find the corporate officers of a shell corporation if they know in which state the shell has been incorporated.

But this makes it sound easy. The shell could have been incorporated in New York state. Unless someone in Las Vegas pulled up the public documents from the corporation file on the State of New York website, the corporation would be invisible. Discovery of the shell is made more complicated by the fact that there are hordes of names like James T. Johnson who have some connection to a corporation on paperwork filed in New York state. Making the connection between the James T. Johnson on the New York paperwork and the James T. Johnson of the Cypress Casino would be very difficult.

Further, if the man in the corporation had a unique name like Moshe P. Varoufakis, the name of a brother-in-law would be used. Or a wife could use her maiden name. Or a close friend who would—beforehand— sign away all rights to or emanating from the shell corporation. (This is known as a "pencil claim.") If the shell really wanted to keep the existence secret, it could incorporate through a New York lawyer's office, and, in that case, only the lawyer's name would appear on the public document on the Recorder's Office web page on the state of New York URL.

Still keeping the example as simple as possible, let us suppose that Bank A and Casino B need to form a shell corporation in St. Louis called ABC Corporation. Keeping the process simple, the board of directors of ABC Corporation will be the bank and casino owners. Now ABC Corporation will establish another corporation, the DEF Corporation, which is a wholly owned subsidiary of ABC Corporation. This is done because a bank official cannot personally profit from a loan in which he is a partner. That is, bank official Joe Smith cannot loan his bank's money to a shell he is associated with and then take $100,000 out as executive pay. But he can get the $100,000 from a subsidiary of that corporation. This is how Bank A board members can profit from their own money. As long as they get their payback from the DEF Corporation, it has been an arm's length financial transaction.

With the intervening corporation, the banks and casino have established an arm's-length mechanism to profit from the real-estate sale. Now, money from the sale of the city blocks would go into the ABC Corporation coffers and thereafter be transferred to the DEF Corporation and the board of directors thereof. This financial slight-of-hand makes everything legal in the eyes of the SEC and the Nevada Gaming Control Board. The bank official can now take his pay and profit legally, with only the IRS being interested in what is now called income.

The second step of the SSS is finding the land and money to buy the two city blocks. This is the *shuffle*. ABC Corporation will get loans—on paper—of a zillion dollars and then try to buy up the needed property. If the property is raw land or in foreclosure, the process is relatively simple. ABC Corporation simply makes an offer to whichever bank holds the title of the raw land or the property in foreclosure. This is how it could work in every city but Las Vegas.

In Las Vegas, a real-estate transaction this size requires secrecy. No one *in* the shell corporation wants anyone *outside* of the shell corporation to know what is going on. So the ABC Corporation will have Bank A transfer the title of the raw land and foreclosed property to its care. To keep everyone guessing, Bank A will buy the raw land and foreclosed property *it wants*, as well as a handful of other lots that have *nothing whatsoever* to do with the two blocks ABC Corporation really needs. These excess lots are the proverbial red herrings. By buying the red herring, ABC Corporation is setting up a false trail for anyone looking to discover and cash in on the real deal.

Sort of.

On one hand, every big casino and bank in Las Vegas participates, has participated, or will participate in some part of an SSS over a period of a few years. So cabals are accumulating property all the time. And selling them. Further, an investment group in New Jersey may be dealing with four or five shell corporations at the same time. The New Jersey investment group does not particularly care where it gets the two city blocks as long as the property is near the Strip. So there could be four or five shells being putting together for a deal that, in the end, may go nowhere at all.

On the other hand, the acquisition of land is a good thing.

For the banks.

Every time a bank picks up title to a piece of property, it is a loss on its books. That is, if Bank A buys the title to a single lot of raw land for $10,000, this is a loss of $10,000 in cash on its books. It has converted cash to land. This reduces Bank A's income by $10,000 and thus has reduced its income tax liability. Then Bank A sells the land to the ABC Corporation for a dollar. The bank's income for that sale is $1. Now the ABC Corporation sells the land to the DEF Corporation for $1. In the Morphean universe, a $10,000 acquisition has been a loss on the books to Bank A, but the $10,000 property—still with a market value of $10,000—has been transferred on paper twice for $1 each time and given the ABC Corporation and the DEF Corporation income of a meaningless $1. Multiply this process by 60, and Bank A will have generated a book loss of $600,000 while legally transferring $600,000 in property to the ABC Corporation and thereafter the DEF Corporation for $60—another meaningless income figure.

Once the ABC Corporation and the DEF Corporation have been established and swell with properties, if the deal goes south, the two corporations still have the collected properties. They also still have a lot of the red herring properties that were bought to throw other investors off the scent. Sooner or later all the properties—one at a time or in groups—can be sold to other shell companies or cashed out.

If there are established businesses on the land being bought, the process is a bit stickier.

Again, keeping the example as simple as possible, if there is a small business within the desired two city blocks, ABC Corporation has to figure out a way to move the owner out. Usually this means offering the business owner more than their business and the land combined are worth. If the business is worth $500,000 and the land $500,000, ABC Corporation might offer $1,250,000. If there are multiple businesses on the lots in need, the ABC Corporation might offer $1.5 million per business as long as all businesses agree to take the offer. If the price is high enough, the business will sell. They should. If you own a small business within a few blocks of the Strip, you know it will only be a matter of time before you are going to be made an offer you cannot refuse. At the same time, the banks love the artificial loss. It converts cash—that can be taxed as income—into property, which is a tax deduction, and reduces income.

There is a lot of upfront money needed in any SSS scheme, and that is why the game is played exclusively by the big boys and girls. Las Vegas is the land of Pie in the Sky, and a lot of these so-called golden opportunities are pyrite. Most of the large companies looking to come to Las Vegas are actually just fishing. If they can get the land they need for a rock-bottom price, yes, they will cut the deal. But their rock-bottom price is usually far less than the real-estate market will bear.

So the deal falls through.

Now the real estate bought is shelved, the third S. There is no longer a need for the ABC and DEF corporations. Maybe they stay in business and wait for the next big deal. Or they are collapsed, and the properties go back to Bank A. If the original deal was for Casino B to be a 50% partner, then 50% of the land goes back to Casino B. But the land value on the books at the DEF Corporation was $1 a lot, so the 30 pieces of property with a market value of $300,000 will go back to Casino B for a book income of a meaningless $30.

Everyone is happy, including the IRS, because all the numbers match.

Over the years and over the deals that have come and not gone, the banks in Las Vegas have accumulated a lot of real estate. But that's perfectly acceptable for three reasons. First, when they bought land, they used actual cash from their retained earnings. The acquisition of the real estate was thus a net *loss* on their balance sheet, which reduced their taxable income. Second, they have turned a *loss* into an asset because they now have real estate with a high value in their portfolio. Third, there will always be another deal out there, and land values in Las Vegas near the Strip have yet to go down. Even if the bank cannot get into the next deal, it could still use the land it has as a bargaining chip.

Now the process gets dicey. Even though banks are not legally allowed to discuss business among themselves, as the expressions goes, "it's been known to happen." Just as there are sub rosa discussions, there are land transfers. One bank helps another by swapping equivalently priced properties. Bank A sells a million-dollar lot to Bank B for $1, and Bank B sells Bank A another lot worth a million dollars for $1. Both banks pay their own mortgage fees and "that's that." With three or four dozen banks in Las Vegas, Reno, and Carson City doing the swapping, no one in the state or federal regulatory agencies really knows what is going on. Topping the mélange, all land transactions are reported to the state of Nevada, and it may take months for a title to officially transfer. Thus, the transfers are happening too fast at the front end for regulators to follow and too slow at the back end for regulators to remember to track. It was a beautiful world—if you were a bank.

It was only when Jigger was made vice-president of Business Mortgage Loans did he become aware of why he had been hired in the first place. Unlike the whippersnappers in the banking classes at the junior college, Jigger had a good grasp of the real world. He knew there was a great deal of difference between what is supposed to happen in the real world and what does actually happen. The examples he gave in class clearly indicated that he understood the need to have an adjustable ethical code while, at the same time, knowing not to get too close to the edge of the law. That, in a nutshell, is what makes a great banker. Anyone can be a good banker, but those people retire with pensions. Bankers with an adjustable ethical code do quite a bit better.

It did not take long for Jigger to decipher the SSS game. Even better from the point of view of the Rutherford Bank and Trust, Jigger did not ask any questions. This gave everyone up the administrative food chain plausible deniability. If anything went wrong, well, if the board of directors did not know what was going on, how could they tell anyone it was in violation of some state or federal regulation or statute?

Within six months of being elevated into the vice-presidency, Jigger was left virtually alone. In this case, *virtually* is the correct word because no one above him wanted to have access to his computer. He was making the bank money by setting up shell corporations, shifting moneys between accounts, and exchanging real-estate paper with other banks. Most importantly, Jigger knew without being told that as long as Rutherford Bank and Trust did not become involved with a casino in any capacity other than as a cash storage facility and dollar-for-dollar specific deposits and withdrawals, state and federal bank regulators would do nothing more than give Rutherford Bank and Trust a quick look every March. As long as nothing popped up on the fiscal radar, no regulator would spend more than two days at the bank—at the most.

Everything was going well for Jigger until Dolores Dobbins came into his life.

CHAPTER 15

LAS VEGAS AND SLEAZE

Las Vegas has no SLEAZE.

Sleaze is something that other cities have.

Not Las Vegas.

Scandal? Yes!

Dirty laundry? Yes!

Schemes and scams? Yes!

Corruption! Yes!

SLEAZE? *No!* Double *no!*

Las Vegas did not have SLEAZE.

SLEAZE was too low class for Las Vegas. Even more important, people did not want to read about SLEAZE.

Scandal? Yes!

Dirty laundry? Yes!

Scheme and scam? Yes!

Corruption! Yes!

SLEAZE? *No!* Double *no!*

If there was any one person who had no trouble understanding that Las Vegas did not have a SLEAZE factor, it was Walter Otterburg, publisher/editor/reporter for *Las Vegas Scandal, Inc.* He and it were the TMZ for Las Vegas. He had to have the facts right but published them like a supermarket tabloid. What was most important for Otterburg was that it was profitable. He had never been successfully sued. Truth is always the best defense.

That being said, when the truth was not clear and unambiguous, a little help is needed.

The evening he got the call about the Howard Hughes codicil, he rolled his eyes. (*Another nutcase. Another wild Howard Hughes conspiracy buff on the phone,* he thought. *Note the look of* surprise *on my face!*) On top of that, the woman was obviously drunk. But when she said she had a copy of the codicil, she went from nut-case category to could-be-legitimate-tip territory.

CHAPTER 16

ZAPATA GETS A PLAN B

There was only one way to describe the former Mrs. Sandoval Wisnoski: psycho bitch from hell. And that label was too soft. She was the kind of woman who made Cruella de Vil seem a martyr and Lady McBeth a saint. She had been born with a single cell of compassion, but it had died in childbirth. She had the sexual drive of an earthworm and had used sex as a lure to get married. Then she went chaste as fast as wedding cake went through her intestinal track. She had numerous kith and kin in Las Vegas, who lived with the couple in a cramped house, believed labor of any kind to be pestilential, and had a worldview that ended at the tip of their nose. She did, however, have her redeeming features. She was one of the best-looking women in Las Vegas even at 55. Her face was naturally beautiful and required no Botox. She had perfect breasts that had not sagged with age, had hips and thighs that rejected fat, and sported legs alluring enough to be used on a James Bond movie poster. Six months after they tied the knot, the only thing she and Bullet had in common was that they had both been married on the same day. After three years of holy matrimony, it was worth every penny Bullet spent to get the woman gone.

Both married and divorced, she had been incredibly expensive. Both married and divorced, Bullet was in the poorhouse. The only silver lining in the cumulonimbus in his life was that the storm was dissipating. What he had to do now was pick up the pieces.

For Bullet, the Frankincense brothel was his respite. Located well away from the Strip and the Triple Pines, it was a place he could go to for the pleasure denied him in his marriage and not be seen by anyone he knew from his work-a-day job. While it was certainly true that the brothel had an extensive menu, for Bullet, conventional sex was his therapy. He had never been a man about town and had hoped that getting married, even late in life, was going to solve what had become a recurring need. He needed sexual release on a regular basis. Single in Las Vegas was a problem if you worked on the Strip. You could not urinate in the well from which you drank, and he didn't need any repercussions at work for his recreational release. Trick-rolling was common, and the last thing he needed was his name on a Las Vegas police report. Worse, at that time there was a strong link between recreational release and drugs. He needed the former but eschewed the latter. He was death on drugs. He had seen too many men go down a very dark road with drugs, both in Vietnam and in Las Vegas. Many of those men had been close friends.

He was a simple man when it came to his pleasures. He needed an occasional lay in a safe brothel, and his regularity at the brothel brought him a measure of companionship. It was not cheap in any sense of the term, but it was worth the price—and no one expected a marriage at the end of a rainbow.

For years, his regular partner was Zapata. Until they became more personally entwined, he only knew her by that name. Usually he called ahead and made an appointment. He and Zapata would share an hour of pleasant sex and then she would go back to the Strip and he would return home. The madam, Frankincense, liked his regularity, and when Zapata was not available, she hooked him up with another of the regulars and occasionally handled the matter herself. In spite of the fact that Frankincense was a confirmed lesbian in a relatively stable relationship, business was, after all, business. This was Las Vegas. Bullet had no problem with having sex with a lesbian; he just wanted the release he needed to keep his mind on his job, not his fantasies.

It was in the Frankincense brothel that Bullet's path crossed that of Jigger again. Jigger didn't plan on getting married. It wasn't that he was against the institution of marriage; he simply could not afford it. Too many of his colleagues had fallen, and he had seen how incredibly expensive it had been for them to recover in both the monetary and emotional sense. Perhaps even more important, his sexual needs were exotic. This is not to say that he was *into* any of the conventional deviances categories that appear on adult websites. He was an experimenter. He was neither straight nor gay. He was tri-sexual; he'd try anything. His personal sexual philosophy was best summed by Mae West, "Between two evils, I always pick the one I've never tried before." While Bullet came to brothel for succor, Jigger came for adventure. Bullet was happy for his hour with Zapata; Jigger wanted to own someone for an hour or two.

It took time for the two men to acknowledge each other in the brothel. The two had crossed paths for years before in the brothel, but it was not until Jigger became the manager of Casino Operations at Rutherford Bank and Trust did the two men have anything in common but high testosterone levels. But after five years of contact at both work and play, the relationship between the men grew to the point that they would causally converse of their life's travails—at the brothel, not on the job.

Sex aside, there was one thing both men had in common, though it would take a crisis to bring them together: both men were not on a fiscal road to anywhere. That is to say, both men were logging time in their respective occupations. They had to work because they could not afford to be unemployed, and they both knew that their approaching retirement was going to be penurious. Such were the wages of honesty. But then, again, both men had witnessed the price of dishonesty. They were still employed while many of their colleagues had fallen by the wayside for a few thousand dollars.

Particularly frustrating, both, independently, had watched their superiors make millions by using the financial system to advantage. It wasn't that these men and women were smarter than Bullet or Jigger, individually or combined. It was that it took money to make money. There was massive chasm between the rich and the poor, and neither man could leap that canyon in a single bound.

All would have gone on as before, but life, alas, does not follow a Hollywood script. It, like God, is unpredictable. The first to realize that her life had to change was Zapata. She was disgusted with the way she was making her living but did not see a Plan B. Every time she considered getting out of the hooking business and looked for that Plan B, she was appalled at her options. Even with a college degree, she would be forced to take a cut in pay by at least half and end up working in a mindless job, always worried that she would be replaced by a younger worker.

But she could not keep doing what she was doing.

The discussion of her future came up frequently in her liaison with Bullet. By this time Bullet considered her a confidante as well as a Tuesday tryster. He would not be brokenhearted to see her leave her profession, but he was in the same circumstance. Something had to happen if she—and he—kept going down similar roads. Bullet did not have a Plan B to suggest. He worked for a casino, and it was from that hellhole she had risen. She was not about to go back.

Then, as said before, life was unpredictable. Bullet happened to lament the fact that his tryster was looking to go straight—"not a double entendre," he laughingly told Jigger—and asked if he had a suggestion that did not involve a casino.

Jigger said real estate. There was good, honest money to be made, and if you were good, you could make a living. But you had to be careful, he advised. Successful realtors make a lot of money, but they also have a lot of expenses. A better idea would be to get into the title business. Every land transaction requires a lot of paperwork. Buying, selling, transferring, swapping, combining, or any combination thereof requires paperwork. If you don't have the money to get into speculating on land, the next best thing is to make money on the speculation. Maybe

Zapata should look at working for a title company. Jigger gave Bullet a few names, and, a month later, Zapata was working part time in a title company office.

But she kept her night job.

CHAPTER 17

JEROME FOLTZ SLIMES INTO THE SCENARIO

Jerome Foltz was a bottom feeder. He didn't have a problem with the label. He *was* a bottom feeder. It was legal. It was part of the business world. It paid well. He had no problem with money. He made a lot of money because he made his employers a lot of money. "Employers" was actually the wrong term. They were "clients." That was how he listed them on his income tax forms, even though they were casinos. When they had a problem, they asked Foltz to "look into the matter." That was all they said. That was all they wanted to say. That was all they needed to say. Foltz was like a private eye but for casinos. He followed the money.

One of his blessings was that he was in Las Vegas. This was not because he had been born and raised in the city or that his parents had both been in the casino business. He was lucky because his bottom feeding was actually done in the upper echelons of the casino business. He wasn't looking for card cheats or armed bandits. That was chicken feed. He was after the people who were after the very big money, the scams and schemes that ran into the millions of dollars. In this enterprise he was doubly blessed. First, the circles in which he worked were very small. Las

103

Vegas may have been a big town, but when it came to the casino movers and shakers, the numbers were in the score, not the thousands. Everyone knew everyone else or knew of them even if they had not shaken a hand. It was not illegal for these movers and shakers to talk among themselves or, for that matter, do business that was not directly connected to their casino. But there was a legal limit to that discussion.

Everyone talked, and one subject that everyone talked about most frequently was real estate. But it was not in the positive, so to speak. That is, buying land for profit was low on their list of ambitions. It was the reverse. They wanted to know who was buying land, and their interest grew in intensity the closer to the Strip the acquisitions became. There was always room for one more casino and one more hotel. It was inevitable that there was going to be at least one more casino and one more hotel. As the number of visitors was constantly increasing, there were going to be more casinos and hotels. It was a fact of life. The current casino owners just wanted Foltz to make sure they knew when suspicious real-estate deals were in the works. Everyone knew of the SSS nature of Las Vegas real estate, and no one wanted to be taken by surprise.

His second blessing was that he could find niches other people did not know existed. As an example, he knew there were three very large big money games in Las Vegas: gambling, banking and real estate. He also knew that the third rail in all these games—individually and collectively—was cash or things that could be converted to cash like credit cards, checks, certificates of deposit. Most of the scrutiny by state and federal regulators, law enforcement, and the IRS was focused on cash. This was fine with Foltz because Las Vegas was seeing less and less cash as the years went on.

But when it came to noncash transfers, the oversight was, at best, superficial. State and federal regulators looked the bank records with an eye to seeing that the numbers matched. If they did, that was that. Real-estate regulators just looked to make sure that all the documents had been signed. Bank regulators did not interact with the real-estate regulators, so a lot of hanky-panky could occur with no one the wiser. This was all done courtesy of what Foltz called "Immunity by Solidarity."

Immunity by Solidarity is the ingrained legal myth that transactions start and finish with payment. Keeping the reality as simple as possible, suppose Bank A and Real Estate company A have a hot lead. A hotel needs a city block near the Strip. Bank A and Real Estate company A form a joint venture and try to get the title to all the land in a city block. Since SSS has been the standard for decades, the joint venture is not going to be able to find a city block near the Strip where the title to all the land within that block is available. There could be six lots of various sizes within the block owned by six different banks. The joint venture would then begin buying up the six lots. For a nuts-and-bolts example of Immunity by Solidarity, suppose Bank B owns Lot 1. Bank A in the joint venture offers to buy Lot 1 at its appraised value—$6 million. Bank B then sells Bank A Lot 1 for $6 million. As far as state and federal bank regulators are concerned, a transaction has been consummated. That finishes the fiscal oversight. As long as all financial requirements for that sale—and only that sale—have been met, it is a legal sale, and no further examination is required.

End of that story.

Now, in real life generally and Las Vegas in particular, Bank B does not want to have $6 million show up on its books. That is called "income," and it will be taxed. So Bank B has to figure out a way to get the actual $6 million cash off its books without losing $6 million of assets to the bank. So Bank B will sell Bank A *another* lot somewhere in Las Vegas for $6 million. Now both banks have a $6 million sale called "income," and a $6 million acquisition called "expense," and the two balance each other out. What the banks have basically done is switched pieces of properties in the real world and washed the acquisitions on the books. As far as the banking regulators are concerned, the fact that Bank A bought Lot 1 from Bank B and then Bank B used the same money to buy another lot somewhere else has nothing whatsoever to do with first transaction. Every transaction is mutually exclusive from every other transaction even if the same money is used.

What Foltz knew, and the bank and real-estate auditors purposefully refused to acknowledge, was that the real story of what was going on was keeping track of land ownership. If a joint venture was trying to quietly buy up a city block near the Strip, Foltz would know when he saw large land transfers near the Strip. When he found such transactions in progress, he would inform his clients. With advance knowledge of the buyout, they could either buy a critical lot and hold out for a good price or settle for a piece of the pie. It was a long-term game, of course, but the money was incredibly large. For his money, all Foltz had to do was keep watching the real-estate transactions in the state of Nevada's Recorder's Office.

He also had a third blessing: his sense of smell. He could detect the glint of opportunity like a coyote picking up the scent of carrion at five miles. He caught a whiff from a lesbian who was working in a land title office. Foltz had worked with her nephew at the Cypress Casino in the old days, so he knew her very casually but not much better than to say "hello." There was good reason for him not to even say "hello" now. He had brutally forced her nephew out of his job because old people should not block the progress of the young. His parting epithet had been a brutal "how do you like them apples?" But that was ancient history. In Las Vegas everyone quickly learns to redact the past. Bygones were bygones primarily because Las Vegas was so large that the chances of two former enemies meeting again were slim.

The lesbian and a friend had settled into a table next to his in the restaurant dining room where he regularly had breakfast every Monday, Wednesday, and Friday after his Group Power workout. The lesbian had commented that she did not know why anyone would be buying up raw land at this time in this economy.

Foltz didn't know either.

But he smelled profit.

So he spent more time than usual in the state of Nevada's Recorder's Office and looked well beyond a few blocks back from the Strip. He found a lot of raw land being bought for a song well back from the Strip but nothing that looked suspicious. What he was looking for was raw land lots that were side by side or adjacent. He didn't find any.

But the lesbian had said that the raw land was being bought.

So who was doing the buying?

And why?

Since he could not trace the land by lot, he decided to see who was buying land. He had the office run a printout of all raw land bought in the last month and got zip. There were too many lots of land being bought and sold by too many people, businesses, and companies to find any pattern.

Then he remembered that the lesbian had worked for a title company. Gambling that she still had the same name as Harold Dobbins, he got a list of title company owners and employees from the Nevada Real Estate Commission. He found her name with Peters Title Company. Back he went to the Recorder's Office and got a list of title transfers within the last three months.

He got some records but he still could not figure out what he had discovered.

The title company had been buying and transferring titles among the employees and thus washing the transactions. The lesbian—her name was Dolores Dobbins, he discovered—along with the owner of the title company, Jean Peters, were buying property in their own names and then selling to another employee. Dolores had a piece of property that she sold to Peters and then Peters sold Dolores another piece of property, so, on the books, both women ended up with each other's property with no income to be taxed.

But this made no sense at all.

Two people transferring property between them didn't earn either of them a dime. They were not buying and selling; they were trading. Further, some of the properties they were buying were raw land, and others were foreclosed property.

Why?

Was anyone else in the firm doing it?

He pulled up the names of all the people in Peters Title Company and got one more name: Myrrh Frankincense. Then he pulled all purchases for Peters for the past year. There was seven. Six of them were sales to Dolores or Myrrh and one from Rutherford Bank and Trust.

Pulling up the purchases for the past year for Dolores Dobbins and Myrrh Frankincense, he also found seven apiece.

Then a new name popped up: Sandoval Wisnoski. Seven for him too. Bullet?

What the hell did Bullet have to do with all this? He'd known Bullet for years. But Bullet was not a real-estate person. Or a banker. He was a thug who was not smart enough to put on a raincoat in a downpour.

What was going on here?

This was going to take some think time, so he took the copies he had discovered and walked across the street to the coffee shop. He purchased a latte and sandwich and sat down at an empty table with a pad of yellow paper and pen. Then he put the purchases in by date.

That made no sense at all.

All he could say for sure was that the initial mortgages from Rutherford Bank and Trust—eight of them—had four clustered in late January and early February and four more in late April and early May all in the previous year.

So what?

CHAPTER 18

HAROLD CHARLES DOBBINS SWITCHES COURTROOMS

If there was any one place Dobbins never expected to be, it was jail. Or prison; jail being a temporary holding pattern, while time in prison was measured in years. He had spent years being meticulous in his work so he would not end up here—where he was.

He'd spent five decades being accurate because he had multitudinous sets of eyes watching his numbers. That didn't bother him. He had seen too many men and women go down because of the skim. So he didn't, and that kept him in good stead with those multitudinous sets of eyes.

Why was he here again?

Waking up in jail was a shock. *I should not be here*, was his first thought. *Why am I here?* was his second. But first thought or second, he was here, in a jail cell with a man who looked like a wallowing hippopotamus. Snored like one too. There was one thing about jail that struck him from his first step into the hoosegow: the smell. It was a mephitis he knew he would never forget.

Breakfast was edible but the noise deafening. Every manner of clunk, clank, rattle, curse, yell, and passing of gas fore and aft could be heard along the corridor. The hippopotamus added his unique acoustical gift to the cacophony and that, with the stench, reminded Dobbins that this was the last place on earth he wanted to spend another hour.

But then, again, why was he here anyway?

At 9:15 a.m., the guards came tramping down the corridor and began handcuffing the inmates individually and then spacing them out along a length of chain. The hippopotamus was the anchor, in both senses of the term, and they were lockstep marched down the corridor through a garage and into a van with bars on its windows. It was a quick trip from there to the Las Vegas courthouse, the inmates jostling back and forth and cursing the driver the whole way.

On the chain in queue, Dobbins was the butt of every joke and jab and took a few kicks along the way. After all, what was a *material witness* doing here? Who was he ratting out? Savin' his own skin, eh? Well, they'd show him. Everyone in queue knew what dropping the dime meant. This guy was nothing more than a snitch. F#%& 'im.

Then things got worse.

Dobbins had been so preoccupied with the overpowering smell and noise of his jail cell and keeping up with the pace of the queue that he had quite forgotten about the reporters who had followed the Las Vegas police car to the police station and had clogged the sidewalk when he was slipped into the underground garage. He may have dismissed them from his mind, but they had not forgotten him. The moment he entered the courtroom, there was an explosion of camera flashes. Three television cameras zoomed in on his face as he lock-stepped over to the double tier of seats. Only when the prisoners were lined up did the guards release them from the central chain—but not the handcuffs.

As soon as the prisoners were seated, the clerk, young enough to be Dobbins's granddaughter—if he had had a granddaughter—stood up and said the court was in session, Honorable James J. Smith presiding. (*James Smith?* thought Dobbins. *What an original name!*)

The honorable came out from behind a vertical screen on the dais and sat down. He fiddled with the papers on his desk as if he were reading them and then looked up. First, he looked at Dobbins—and it was a direct look at Dobbins—and then at the crowd. The courtroom was chockablock with spectators, packed so full that to Dobbins it appeared that there were two tiers of heads, one from those seated and the other from those standing. A lot of faces looked familiar, news people from morning and evening shows, and in the front—front and center—were the three pasty-haired, starch-white, mousey IRS agents who had been at his doorstep. He was in state court, Dobbins mused; what were they doing here?

That was exactly the question the Honorable James J. Smith had. Lifting up a sheet of paper as if it had vermin attached, he asked why the case of one Harold Charles Dobbins was in his court. A man young enough to be Dobbins's grandson—if he had had one—stood up from the chair at the side of the prosecutor's table in the front of the chamber and solemnly walked toward the podium. He had a puzzled look on his face. Before he had a chance to speak, the three IRS agents stood up, and one of them—the one Dobbins could not determine—said, "If it please the court!"

The honorable against shook the foolscap. "Does it relate to the case of Harold Charles Dobbins?"

"Yes, your honor."

"Then, no, it does not please the court. Please be seated. Mr. Hastings, why is this dog in my courtroom?"

"Dog, your honor?" The young man at the podium was taken aback.

"Dog, Mr. Hastings, dog." The honorable shook the foolscap again. "What I see here is that Mr. Dobbins is being held as a material witness in a federal case, yet he is in my court. Again, Mr. Hastings, why is Mr. Dobbins in my courtroom?"

"May it please the court," tried one of the IRS agents again.

"It does not," snapped the honorable. "If you say it again, I will hold you in contempt. Do I make myself clear?"

There was some grumbling, and the IRS agents sat down.

"Now, Mr. Hastings, let me get this straight. Mr. Dobbins is being held in the Las Vegas city jail as a material witness for the United States government because he is allegedly knowledgeable of an alleged

111

missing fifty million dollars from the late Howard Hughes who may or may not have left the money to a woman who may or may not have been his first wife."

"Yes, your honor."

The honorable looked up as if he were seeking guidance from heaven. "Though you are a young man, Mr. Hastings, I am sure that living in Las Vegas, you must have come across the name of Howard Hughes in your ancient history class."

"Yes, your honor, you see . . ."

"I will do the talking, Mr. Hastings."

Hastings choked on a "Yes, your honor."

The honorable shook the foolscap again. Then he turned it on end and pointed it at Hastings. "This is a dog, Mr. Hastings. A dog, Mr. Hastings, is something that howls at the moon to frighten away spirits that do not exist. There is not a shred of probable cause here—or even improbable cause. I have been on this bench longer than you have been at the bar, and this, sir, is a dog. Worse, it is clear that for some reason the city of Las Vegas and the state of Nevada have been asked to carry water for the United States government because the case is so weak." He stopped, as it was clear that Hastings was about to say something. "Don't say a word, Mr. Hastings."

Hastings stopped before his sentence started.

"Now, Mr. Hastings, let me get this straight. All I want you to do is answer yes or no when I ask you a question, is that clear?"

Hastings nodded.

"No, Mr. Hastings. I asked you say yes or no when I ask a question. Is *that* clear?"

"Yes, your honor."

"Thank you. Mr. Dobbins is being held in the Las Vegas city jail as a material witness?"

"Yes, your honor."

"Then it goes without saying that he must be being held because of a matter that involves the city of Las Vegas, Clark County or the state of Nevada."

"Yes, your honor."

"As I read this, this, this," said the honorable as he shook the paper, "dog, Mr. Dobbins is being held on the recommendation of the United States government represented by the Internal Revenue Service of being a flight risk because he may have hidden fifty million dollars from a will that may or may not be a forgery from Howard Hughes who has been dead for more than fifty years to a woman who was never his first wife. Is that correct?"

"Yes, your honor, but . . ."

"Mr. Hastings, I told you to say only yes or no. Is that correct?"

"Yes, your honor."

"Even if these allegations are true, Mr. Hastings, which I find as reasonable as Elvis being on a spaceship with the Loch Ness Monster, there are a lot of problems here. First, there is not a shred of prima facie evidence—evidence, Mr. Hastings, evidence—that this alleged document exists. Further, even if such a codicil did exist and is genuine, then the money involved is called inheritance, and that, as far as I know, is still legal within this city, county, state, and nation. Am I correct, Mr. Hastings?"

"Yes, your honor."

"It's good to see we are on the same wavelength, Mr. Hastings. Now, moving along, even if the will is phony, and the money was stolen, the statute of limitations on every aspect of this case has run out. So, Mr. Hastings, why is Mr. Dobbins being held as a material witness?"

"Well, your honor," said Hastings, but before he could continue, IRS Agent Titterington, the agent who had questioned Dobbins in his home, was on her feet again. "May it please the court!"

"Yes, now it does please the court. Please state your name for the record and standup comedians to use this evening."

If the snide comment bothered Titterington, she gave no indication.

"Your honor, I am IRS Agent Jane Titterington."

"Yes, Ms. Titterington. Proceed."

"Within the last two days, it came to the attention of the IRS that there was a plausible case of fraud involving Mr. Dobbins. We were provided with a Xerox of a codicil that named a Jean Peters as the recipient of fifty million dollars in cash. That Ms. Peters was the first wife of Howard Hughes. The money went to the wrong Ms. Peters. Ms. Peters who should have received the codicil is deceased."

"Which Ms. Peters should have gotten the money? Howard Hughes's first wife or the woman who was not his wife?"

"Ms. Peters—that was his wife—is deceased. The Ms. Peters who was not his wife is in the wind."

"This is rich, Agent Titterington; please proceed."

"It appears that the Ms. Peters who was not Howard Hughes's first wife had apparently received money that should have been given to the real wife of Howard Hughes . . ."

"How do you know that, Agent Titterington?"

"Your honor?"

"Even if the money existed, how do you know for a fact that Howard Hughes left the Jean Peters who *was not* his wife money that should have been given to the Jean Peters *who was* his first wife?"

"It's . . . it's just reasonable, your honor."

"It is not reasonable, Agent Titterington. Nothing that has been presented in this court today on this matter is reasonable. But let's just cut to the chase, Agent Titterington. I have to assume that Mr. Dobbins is being held in a city facility as a material witness at your request. Is that correct?"

"Yes, your honor."

"Why isn't Mr. Dobbins being held in a federal facility or, even better, why not in the honeymoon suite at the Bellagio under around-the-clock guard by the forces of truth, justice, and the American way?"

"Well, your honor."

"Let me guess. The arrest took place on a Sunday, and every federal judicial figure with brains was unreachable."

"I resent the characterization being made with regard . . ."

The honorable shook the foolscap. "I resent this dog ending up on my desk. Now, let's get down to brass tacks. Mr. Dobbins has violated no city, county, or state statute or regulation. He is being held as a courtesy to the United States government as a material witness in a federal matter that only . . ." The honorable stalled for a moment. Before he could begin again, a man old enough to actually remember Howard Hughes jumped up from a seat in the back of the room.

"May it please the court!"

"This is getting tiresome. Who are you?"

"Temporary Assistant United States Attorney for the state of Nevada."

"Do you have a name?"

"Yes, your honor, but as I actually work out of the Los Angeles office of the United States Attorney, so my name will not be listed in the employees of the United States Attorney staff in Nevada."

"Are you licensed to practice in Nevada?"

"No, your honor."

"Then sit down and shut up."

The white-haired lawyer sat down, and a jack-in-the-box lookalike jumped up.

"May it please the court!"

"Let me guess. You are with the United States Attorney's office in Nevada, and you are licensed to practice law in Nevada?"

"Yes, your honor."

"I must be psychic. Proceed whatever your name is."

"Your honor, there was no one available in the United States Attorney's office on Sunday, yesterday, so Agent Titterington persuaded the Las Vegas police to detain Mr. Dobbins as a material witness until such time as we could arrange to have him detained as a federal material witness. We believed then—and now—that he is a flight risk."

"Using the Las Vegas police as kind of a holding pattern?"

"Well, your honor, that's not . . ."

"That's the way it looks to me. I will not have my court used as an extension of the lunacy of the federal government. According to the document in my possession," he shook the foolscap again, "Mr. Dobbins has committed no act to get himself held as a material witness. So I am releasing him . . ."

Hastings cut in. "There is a resisting arrest charge outstanding."

"Mr. Hastings, pleeeaaaasssee. You are being used by the feds. Let them do their own dirty work. Mr. Dobbins is free to go." To the bailiff he said, "Release Mr. Dobbins immediately, personally escort him to the city jail to retrieve his belongings, and take him home with apologies from the city of Las Vegas, Clark County, and the state of Nevada."

Dobbins stood up and stretched his arms outward so the bailiff could unlock his handcuffs. Just as Dobbins stood, another man in the crowd stated above the hubbub, "May it please the court!"

"And who are you?"

"I am also from the United States Attorney's office. I have a warrant for Mr. Dobbins to be held as a federal material witness." The man waved a folded sheet of paper overhead.

"So now the *feds* want to hold Mr. Dobbins as a material witness?"

"We were only able to get a federal warrant this morning."

"All the federal judges out playing golf yesterday? Interesting. Let me see the paperwork." After reading the writ, the honorable turned to Dobbins. "Mr. Dobbins it seems that you are being dragged from pillar to post. My apologies to you, sir. This is not the way the state of Nevada does business. All I can do is dismiss your case with prejudice, but you will have to go with this gentleman," he said, indicating the United States Attorney with writ in hand. "This dog is now in federal court."

The honorable hit his desk with a gavel. "Court will recess for fifteen minutes."

Again, at the focus of flashing cameras and rolling television cameras, Dobbins was released from the state of Nevada handcuffs and placed in the U.S. handcuffs and escorted out the back of the courtroom.

"Someone sure dropped a dime on you!" shouted the hippopotamus as the door closed behind Dobbins.

CHAPTER 19

THE LAS VEGAS
PUSHMI-PULLYU

Born in 1886 in Maidenhead, Berkshire, in January 1886 to English and Irish parents, Hugh Lofton expected his life to be one of sedate, middle-class living. He had received his college degree in England and then spent two years at MIT studying to become an engineer. All seemed to be moving along swimmingly until a man in Bosnia-Herzegovina had the misfortune to get between the clear blue sky and the muzzle of a pocket-sized FN Model 1910 pistol with .380 ACP cartridges. The man was Franz Joseph, and his death led to the First World War.

Lofton enlisted in the Irish Guard and, at 28, found himself in the trenches. He was to stay in the trenches for the duration of the war, four years of a living hell where he never knew from hour to hour if he was going to live until the next sunrise. Before the war ended, he would be seriously wounded and come close to death.

Married and with children, he could not bring himself to write to his family of the insane slaughter that was occurring hourly on the Western Front. So he created an artificial world and sent his children letters with illustration of a veterinarian living in the fictional English village

117

of Puddleby-on-the-Marsh. The veterinarian had the unique talent of being able to speak to the animals in their own tongues. The stories of the fabled Dr. Doolittle included such characters as a monkey by the name of Chee-Chee, an owl named Too-Too, a pig named Gub-Gub, and the Pushmi-pullyu. The last of these was a cross between a unicorn and a gazelle, with a head of each animal at either end of its body. The name, of course, implies that if the unicorn half of the body moved forward, the gazelle half must necessarily move backward.

Though Lofton died in 1947, his characters have lived on in movies, television serials, and Sunday comic strips. But only one character was able to leap from the comics to the real world: the Pushmi-pullyu. Half a century after his death, the Pushmi-pullyu made it into the lexicon of the real world. It made its entrance in the political campaign industry. With some adjustment to the original intent of the animal, the Pushmi-pullyu became the symbol for the driving force of a winning political campaign. The key to political success was to drive home a succinct message to the voters: you should vote for this candidate (the pull) and, at the same time, why you should *not* vote for the opponent (the push). This theme then became the main thrust of every campaign in all speeches, handouts, radio advertisements, television commercials, and endorsements.

The Pushmi-pullyu made it into general usage as a way of implying that someone arrived at a decision because of circumstances, not by free will. "Free will" is a generic term that implies that someone made a decision when the alternatives were equally desirable—or equally detestable. Julie had a choice of marrying Joe or George, and she chose Joe. She may later regret the choice—and tell Joe about it for decades—but at the moment of her choice, it was a matter of free will.

The Pushmi-pullyu is different because it implies the choice is made because there are powerful forces *pushing* for a conclusion with other forces, at the same time pulling toward a resolution. A pregnancy, for instance, creates a *pushing*. It is a life-changing matter that requires a woman to make critical, life-changing choices. At the same time, if the pregnant woman is single, not in a serious relationship, over 30, and in the working class, she will be pulled into a myriad of ways depending on the push. She can have an abortion, force a casual relationship to become serious, find a suitable relationship where the man is willing to accept another man's child, have the child and put it up for adoption, return to her parents' home and raise the child, or have and keep the child and live as a single working mother. She is being pushed and pulled at the same time, thus the Pushmi-pullyu.

In December 1972, that was the Pushmi-pullyu Dolores Dobbins faced. She was a single card dealer, 32 years of age, and in a casual relationship. A *very casual* relationship. Unfortunately—or, as with 20-20 hindsight, fortunately—the casual relationship was with a married man. That was the good news. The bad news was that he was a pilot for Trans World Airlines and was in and out of town in both senses of the term; had a wife who knew of her husband's philandering (in the multiples), his illegitimate offspring (in the plural), and his habit of living large on his TWA salary—across the United States—and that it was her family money that kept him from personal bankruptcy and ending up living on Social Security. His decision was not hard to make; he never called her again.

Her personal decision was a bit stickier. In 1975, abortion was illegal in most parts of the United States in general and in Nevada in particular. *Roe v. Wade* was still a year away, but in the United States that was not called "the Deep South"; abortions were performed with regularity in safe medicinal settings. They were called, among other things, "medical procedures." The key to understanding abortions in those days was not what the procedure was called; it was how it was paid for. The more you could pay, the less invasive it was. If you were not in the working class and could pay, it was a relative humane operation. If your income level was lower than that, well, things could get very complicated and very deadly. Dolores was lucky because she was employed. There was a Planned Parenthood clinic in Las Vegas in those days, and "arrangements" were made "that facilitated the medical procedure." It was painful but of short duration.

For every woman an abortion leaves scars, if not physical at least psychological. No matter how she views the procedure, there is still the undeniable fact that life in some rudimentary form was involved. Regardless of the circumstances, there are regrets that do not ameliorate over the years. Even in the case of a Finkbine, there will be second, third, and fourth thoughts long after the event. Never having had the opportunity to have a child is one thing; tossing the possibility aside is another.

Dolores was like many women who were faced with a difficult life choice. She could not afford a child, was not mature enough to be a mother, did not have a lifestyle conducive to raising a child on her own, had seen a progression of foster children at her church when she was growing up, and, most important, understood she needed a long-term stable relationship in her life with or without a child. At that moment she had zip in the relationship category.

There was also another matter for her to consider. That was her sexuality. In those days and the present, the prevailing belief is that the world is composed of two categories of sexual lifestyles: "normal," which usually means "straight," and "deviant," which is everything else. This is a manifestation of the human being that has no basis in reality. Everyone is kinky in their own way; "straight" people do indulge in fantasy sexual antics, and "deviant" people often have long-term loving relationships. Straight people who attend orgies once or twice in their lifetime are not considered "deviant," while a single person who does the same is so considered. Many gay men are happily married to women. Many lesbians have husbands. Bisexual men and women in relationships do not look at themselves as "deviant" and often have children who accept them for what they are. Even more important, gay and lesbian couples raise children who do not "turn out" to be gay, while heterosexual couples sometimes have children who grow up to be gay or lesbian. At best, life is a crapshoot. All you can do is throw the dice and live with the consequences.

Dolores did not look at the abortion as a major turning point in her life. It was an unfortunate low spot but not a game changer by any means. But it did open her eyes to a very real aspect of her future: she was going nowhere. It was not as if she believed she had a biological clock that was ticking. More precisely, she knew there was a clock ticking, but it was with regard to what she was doing with her life. She was making the same amount of money at 32 that she had been making at 22. If she was not careful, she'd be making the same amount of money doing the same thing at 42 that she was doing now. The only difference was that the tips might not keep up with inflation.

More importantly, she realized that the people with whom she was working had the IQ of a gerbil. They may have been incredibly good-looking courtesy of modern medicine, but unless they hooked a rich husband, they were going to be on the same treadmill as she was running. She found school boring and could not see a profession that made her heart beat fast.

The product of a large extended family whose members had expired early, scattered to the wind or were in the wind, she only had one relative with whom she was close. That was her nephew Harold. Harold had actually finished college and was working as an accountant at the Cypress Casino. He was not very high up in the organization, but he had moxie and brains. He was about to go somewhere—just not yet. He was too young.

But he was not too young to understand where Dolores was *not going*. Even in his short time in the casino on the floor and then in the counting room, he had seen enough to know that Dolores had to get off the treadmill she was on. He did not have a good idea of where she should be headed, only that he knew Dolores was on the wrong road. He had no specific suggestion for her as to what to do. All he had was the name of an older acquaintance at the Triple Pines, a man he knew was steering clear of even the hint of impropriety. He was going through a rough time with his on-again-off-again wife who was jerking him through legal hoops like a water-skier on an obstacle course. Maybe his friend Bullet could give her some advice.

CHAPTER 20

TUESDAY AFTERNOON WITH PROF

Tuesday afternoon's class was abuzz with the previous Monday's court session where Dobbins slid out of state court only to be snagged into federal court. The general feeling was that some people never get a break. This week Dobbins had made it from pan to fire, and everyone conceded that they had no idea what was actually going on. Why was Dobbins being held at all? Better yet, what was Prof going to saying about the codicil today? After all, the breaking news in the state court had already come and gone, and the hearing before the federal judge was this afternoon. There was no hot news to report.

But Prof had been rolling lectures over in his head for two days. Unlike other instructors at the junior college, he had no notes. He hated lecture notes. When he had used them, he stuck to the script. When he stuck to the script, he was historically accurate, included all the nuances of the era of which he was lecturing, and students had not learned a goddamn thing. That was because the students could not see a link between what was being taught in class and what was happening in their real world. So he scrapped his notes and went wild, mixing the b-o-r-in-g eat-your-peas-because-they-are-good-for-you lectures, which linked the real world that the students knew, with the historical lessons they should know. After all, he said so many times that students recited the mantra out loud in class: "History is not the story of the past; it is the study of the future."

So what rabbit was he going to pull out of his hat today?

Prof loved surprises.

He began his lecture that morning about some English writer no one had ever heard of. This guy had been born in Bromley, Kent—which sounded like a joke—and had been apprentice to a draper. A draper, Prof had to explain, was basically a person who sold cloth. Cloth as in fabric. A draper would wholesale fabric to other businesses who would turn the cloth into drapes, shirts, trousers, underwear, handkerchiefs and whatever else. This Englishman got tired of fabric, so he became a teacher of biology—and that was quite a switch. Tired of teaching, he tried his hand at writing. He was substantially more successful as a writer and switched his name from Hebert George to H. G. With his initials instead of his first two names, H. G. Wells went on to write groundbreaking science-fiction works, which were still being read a century later. Even more important, he was one of the few "ancient" writers whose work had leaped from the manuscript page to the silver screen.

Even when he told the students the name of H. G. Wells, there was a blank stare from 99% of the students, because only one in 50 knew that Tom Cruise had starred in *War of the Worlds*, and he, the student, remembered that H. G. Wells was credited as the creator of the story in some pop magazine. But he, the same student, had only half-remembered, so that drove the 98% to 99%.

Prof noted that H. G. Wells had also written *The Time Machine*, *The Island of Doctor Moreau*, and *The Invisible Man*. *The Time Machine* had been turned into so many movies, television presentations, comic books, radio theaters, and sci-fi movies—not to mention television advertisements—that all the students had passing understanding of the concept. Not so much *The Island of Doctor Moreau*. Prof had to clarify that Wells's *The Invisible Man* had been turned into many movies, of

123

which *Hollow Man* with Kevin Bacon, *Memoirs of an Invisible Man* with Chevy Chase, and *The Invisible Man* animated series on television were not among them. Neither was Ralph Ellison's *Invisible Man*.

When someone asked why Prof was talking about a British writer who had been dead for almost a century, Prof stated that the Wells had come up with a novel concept of time that he wanted to discuss. As Wells wrote in *The Time Machine*, physical objects actually had four dimensions: length, breadth, width, and time. What he had meant was that an apple that you can see only exists as that apple for that split second in eternity. A week from now, that apple will not be the same. Time changes it. This concept is nothing new. Heraclitus of Ephesus, 535–475 BC E, famously stated that you cannot step in the same river twice. What he meant was that everything was changing—and changing so fast—that by the time you took your second step in any river, the river was not the same as it was when you put your first foot in.

In real life, Prof went on, every object has more than four dimensions. Yes, it has length, width, and breadth along with time, but it also has a functional dimension. A fish, for instance, can be eaten, stuffed and hung on a wall, used to stock a lake, or feed to a dog. It can be an ugly fish or a large fish or a fat fish or a spiny fish or an aggressive fish or a fish that walks on land. The world is very Einsteinian, in the sense that every physical object has multiple dimensions in both time and space.

There are also functionalities in the negative, Prof continued. A good example would be using sunscreen in a dark room. Sunscreen, as is the lotion one uses to avoid sunburn, has a real-life purpose. But not in a dark room. The term "dark room" took many students by surprise because in the present day and age, "dark rooms" no longer existed in the photographic sense. Most of the students understood the implication but, in their minds, substituted "a room that is dark, as in unlit," which they could visualize, while the anachronistic photographic darkroom was beyond their cultural experience.

Other functionalities in the negative Prof discussed were motion, shape shifting, and deterioration. With regard to motion, a particle of water in a cloud is spherical. Even though it is stable in the sense that it is still in a cloud, as more and more water vapor transubstantiates into liquid water, the particle becomes larger. When the spheres of water become too heavy to remain in the cloud, by the millions they fall to earth as rain. When the water is in the clouds, it is spherical in form, but the moment it falls to the earth, the air forces the water to become raindrops, which are not spherical. When the raindrops hit the ground, they flatten and run together to form rivulets, streams, rivers, and eventually oceans—until the water deteriorates into vapor that rises to the clouds to begin the process again. Every step of this process involves water, but the forms of the water—length, breadth, height, and time of existence— constantly change.

Just as his students' eyes were about to glaze over, Prof pulled out the morning's newspaper. He pointed to a collection of pictures in the paper and told the students that they were being seduced by the perfection of the moment. Then he explained.

In the study of history as it is now being taught and in newspapers, the emphasis is on snapshots of reality. Prof said he called it the "seduction of the perfect moment." Specifically, he stated as he held up the newspaper and pointed to one of the handful of pictures of Howard Hughes, "These pictures were not taken by accident. None of the pictures in this newspaper were. They were all carefully orchestrated." He specifically pointed to a shot of Howard Hughes next to a plane. Prof said that Howard Hughes wanted to look *exactly* this way for the photographer. "Hughes set up the perfect moment, and the photographer snapped it. Now, half a century later, this is what we will remember that Howard Hughes looked like. That's what Hughes wanted. He wanted this photograph," Prof tapped the newspaper, "to be the eternal image of Howard Hughes. It was his sales pitch.

"An excellent example of the perfect moment," Prof suggested, "is how actors and actresses appear on the red carpet on Oscar night. None of them looked that way the day *before* the event, and none of them would look that way *a week after* the event. But on the night of the Oscars, they want to look their best because that is the way they want movie-goers to believe they look that way all the time. They sell themselves as a visual commodity. Stripped of makeup, fancy clothing, and skin cream, they are just the rest of us: pretty normal looking. But they are not on the red carpet to show they are normal. They have made themselves exotic for the night, their perfect moment for the cameras.

"In real life," Prof continued, "when you open your Sunday newspapers and see all those photographs of the Realtors, how many of those Realtors still look like their photos? Not a lot of them. Most of those pictures are very old. But that doesn't matter to the Realtors. They know people do not buy homes from newspaper or magazine ads. They buy homes from people, flesh-and-blood human beings who can feel their specific needs in a home. The portrait of the Realtor is supposed to convey sympathy, understanding, and professionalism. The Realtor may be none of those, but the picture presents it.

"What does this have to do with history? When you are being seduced by the perfect moment, be keenly aware that there is a lot more going on than the picture implies. The photograph of a confident murderer going to trial saying with sincerity that he is innocent does not mean that he *is* innocent. He just wants you to believe that he is. If he can convince you through the television lens, then he just might be able to convince one juror—and all it takes is one juror—that he *is* innocent. He doesn't need the vote of every juror, just one.

"Do not be seduced by the perfect moment.

"Do your research.

"Read your history.

"Unfortunately, the way history is being taught in *normal* classes," Prof gave a kind of a snarl when he said the word "normal," "it is taught by snapshot. There is a photograph of Abraham Lincoln, and on the next three pages, his life and administration are summed up. That tells you nothing important for your real life. What you want to learn from Lincoln is how he was able to make unpopular decisions that happened to be right. Anyone can make a bad decision just because it is popular. But a real leader makes a tough choice that then shows that it was the right choice. That's why his face is on Mt. Rushmore.

"There is always a lot more going on than what is presented to you in that perfect moment.

"As an example from Las Vegas history," Prof went on to say, "if you were to ask anyone in America who did not go to Las Vegas what they knew about Las Vegas (other than the gambling), they would probably say, 'The shows.' If you asked them which show in particular, the vast majority of those who have never been to Las Vegas would say, 'The Rat Pack.' Then they would say how they remembered watching film clips of the group that included Frank Sinatra; Dean Martin; Sammy Davis, Jr.; Peter Lawford; and Joey Bishop performing on stage. That is their snapshot, their perfect moment.

"The reality is that there is a lot more to the Rat Pack than those five men in 1965 in a thirty-second film clip. There is also a lot of important history to learn from the Rat Pack.

"The real Rat Pack started in the 1950s, and the original leader was Humphrey Bogart. The name originated when Bogart's wife, Lauren Bacall, commented that when Bogart and his friends returned from a romp in Las Vegas, they 'look like a goddamn rat pack.' After that it was called the 'Holmby Hills Rat Pack,' Holmby Hills being where Bogart and Bacall lived.

"The name was reduced to just 'Rat Pack' after Bogart died in 1957.

"But the original Rat Pack was quite large. Even more important, it was influential. In those days the movie moguls controlled the lives of the actors, and the mob controlled the casinos that hired the singers. To get work in the good casinos and with the good movie producers, you had to have connections. The Rat Pack was the connection for these superstars. They worked together, as a unit, and had each other's back. They made a lot of money, yes, but they made money because they worked as a team, not as individuals. A lot of people saw Sinatra, Martin, and Sammy alone. But what was memorable was when they were all together.

"The Holmby Hills Rat Pack was a galaxy of the best stars, including Nat King Cole, Mickey Rooney, Jerry Lewis, Errol Flynn, Caesar Romero, Judy Garland, David Niven, Katharine Hepburn, and Spencer

Tracy among many others. These stars partied together, acted together, and helped each other get parts on the silver screen and in Las Vegas.

"In the 1960s, after the death of Bogart, the focus of the group shifted to Las Vegas rather than Hollywood. That was where the big money was for individual performers. Casino managers loved booking any one of the Rat Packers because they knew if they booked one, a lot of others would show up. The casinos even used the *possibility* of some of the Rat Packers showing up in their marquee. A famous Sands' marque, which can be found on Wikipedia, reads "DEAN MARTIN - MAYBE FRANK - MAYBE SAMMY." The Rat Pack was good for Las Vegas, and Las Vegas was good for the Rat Pack. High rollers came from around the world on the chance that the Rat Pack would be on stage. Their shows sold out, the hotels were packed, and liquor sales went through the roof.

"The historical poin here," Prof told his class, "is that the portrait of Howard Hughes in the newspaper, the photograph of Abraham Lincoln in your history textbook, and the film clip of the Rat Pack are just a snapshot in time. Behind each of these 'perfect moments' was a lot of planning. History and real life were not lived snapshot by snapshot. What a snapshot should be doing is opening up your mind to other possibilities. These snapshots should spark your curiosity. But the snapshot was not real life; it was the perfect moment chosen by the actor, singer, or troupe.

"As a here-and-now example," Prof went on, "the newspapers, television, and radio stations are stumbling over themselves covering Harold Dobbins. It is the story of the moment, a snapshot of history, so to speak. But there is a heck of a lot more going on out there with regard to Dobbins. There is something very big going on in the background. Look at what is going on with hard, cold eyes. Harold Dobbins was a nobody until last week. Now he is front and center in the public's eye. Why?

"Why is the IRS chasing someone based on a document it does not even have? Why are the courts—state and federal—involved? Where is Jean Peters? Even if she is in Manilla, she can be reached. After all, it's her money. So why is Harold Dobbins involved? Why is he worthy of more than a newspaper filler? This is one of those moments when the public is being seduced by the perfect moment. Someone wants us to concentrate on Harold Dobbins.

"Why?

"History has taught us that perfect moment seduces us and keeps us from looking behind the scenes. Like the Wizard of Oz, he does not want us looking behind the curtain. That's the point of the perfect moment. Something very big is happening behind the scenes with regard to Harold Dobbins. What I do not know," Prof told his class, "but believe me, speaking as an historian, when you are being distracted, there is a very good reason your attention has been diverted."

CHAPTER 21

BENNY THE ODDS MAKER

Benny was a bookie.

Benny loved being a bookie.

He had been a bookie for so long that he had a table named after him—Benny the Bookie's table. It was in the restaurant of the Cypress Casino. If you wanted to find Benny, you just went to his table and made the bet. Sports, horseracing, whether the sun would rise, Benny took your bet.

Benny was good with numbers—89 to 5, 7 to 9, whatever. These were the chances of teams winning, horses placing, or the sun coming up. Benny didn't take bets on the sun coming up. He also didn't take bets on the Hughes codicil being legitimate. He didn't take money on a joke. None of the other bookies were taking money on the codicil either. It could be said that it was the first time in Las Vegas history that a bookie didn't take a fool's money.

CHAPTER 22

BULLET MAKES A CONNECTION

The Republican presidential debate in Las Vegas on October 18, 2011, was best described by Bullet as a clusterf#%&. If there was anyone who understood exactly what a clusterf#%& was, it was a Vietnam vet. World War II vets were known as SNAFU and Korean War vets as FUBAR. In 2011, the Republican field was more of a clown car rather than a collection of serious candidates. Newt Gingrich was leading in the polls with 37% of the vote followed by Romney with 25%. Six weeks later Newt was at 6% behind Rick Perry, Sarah Palin, and Ron Paul. Herman Cain was surging at 17%, and Michele Bachman had a solid hold on the lunatic fringe. It was hard to believe that any of these candidates had what it took to be president. Obama may not have been a godsend, but compared to these halfwits, he was head and shoulders above anyone in the Republican pack.

At the same moment, Bullet was finally free of the staggering debt from his ex-wife. She was finally gone and so were the monthly bills that had buried him for a decade. Now he was slowly regaining his financial stability. His wages at the Triple Pines had not improved much, and his lifestyle had gone from modest to worse. He was working a rotating six-day-a-week schedule. His only pleasure was the weekly meeting with Zapata. Both were in their upper sixties now, and he met with her frequently in her hideaway cabin in the Las Vegas badlands. They were both pleased with the trysts because, at their age, sex was their only vice. But a vice it was not, a necessity it was. Sex was the only earthly pleasure that sustained them.

Of the five who met frequently for sex and relaxation, Zapata was doing the best. But it was not a lucrative best. She had stumbled into the title business as a way to leave hooking. She had taken a substantial cut in income, but it had been a great relief to be out of the flesh industry. She did not miss the nightlife and got just enough sex to sustain her sanity. In terms of money, she was doing well enough to be buying her own modest home in the suburbs and this cabin in the wilderness. She was unwittingly benefiting from the SSS days of Las Vegas. While the big boys and girls were trading properties back and forth, she was taking a modest retainer from each transaction. It was modest but consistent. She found it unbelievably boring, but as she had no Plan B, that was where she was.

Her professional life had been made substantially better with arrival of a part-time employee, Harold Dobbins, who had been a political squeeze-out from the Cypress Casino. Dobbins, the nephew of another employee, Delores, had a college degree in accounting, had five decades' experience in the casino industry, and thrived on the meticulous work of the title company. He had started as an occasional worker and was soon doing most of the drudgery work at the title company. Oddly, he enjoyed the mindless work. That was fine with Zapata, she didn't.

Harold Dobbins had been a gift, so to speak, of her only employee: Dolores. Dolores had come to her courtesy of her brothel madam Myrrh. Both Myrrh and Dolores had transitioned from men only to a live-in lifestyle that might have been called lesbian, but they called comfortable. Myrrh still ran the brothel but took one day a week off to be with Peters, Dolores, and Bullet.

Rounding off the uneven number was Jigger, the only one who had no personal catastrophes in his life. He had maintained a once-a-week tryst with the other four for the past ten years. He was still working at

Rutherford Bank and Trust in the same job at the same wage. Banks, like Las Vegas and America in the decade, was cursed with a growing gap between the rich and the poor. The banks were no different. Upper management made incredibly large bucks, while the people in the banking trenches who did the work were poorly paid. It was expected that they would profit from their experience at the bank and move into upper management in the casinos. This was nothing more than a pipedream, an excuse, to underpay. In reality, there was no room for them in upper management in banks or casinos. The good jobs in the casinos went to people with connections, not brains and talent. There were no good jobs in the bank. So Jigger had stayed at Rutherford Bank and Trust, year after year. His lifestyle was less that he wanted, but it was stable.

The only pleasure the five had were the weekly trysts at the cabin where they indulged their ids in whatever combination was most appealing that week. None of the five philandered out of the tribal unit, so there was no fear of STDs or HIV. They did not look at the pairing, tripling, or group romps as deviant or forbidden. It was just the way it was, a physical release from their pressure-cooker lives of their six-day-a-week hell. It had been going along so long that it had become the norm. They had fallen into a rut, so to speak, and none of them wanted out or something new.

Viewed from the outside, the group looked to be nothing more than flabby grandparents who dressed well for work and spent their evenings in pajamas watching *Dancing with the Stars*, wishing they were 40 pounds lighter and 30 years younger. They were so old and conventional looking that they could not have given away film clips of their orgies. No one at Rutherford Bank and Trust or the Triple Pines would have believed that Bullet and Jigger had the energy for a bedroom romp once a year much less weekly. For Jean Peters, the sex was a matter of blowing steam rather than a trip down memory lane, and the general assumption in the Realtor community was that Dolores and Myrrh were the kind of a couple who were more than pleased with each and did not stray because they did not want to strain a fairy-tale relationship, as they expected to live "happily ever after." None of the five had been within

133

walls of an opera house or theater in decades, and the last concert any of them had attended was the reunited Andrew Sisters in 1956. All of them considered the radio to be a waste of time and television, at its best, as mind numbing as their jobs. Their collective range of enthusiasm in their working lives was a flat line.

Sex was thus their only sin. Each of the five had seen the ravages of alcohol, drugs, gambling, and hedonism up close. Each had passed through their years of personal hell dealing with addiction, perversion, physical trauma, in-laws, outlaws, cardsharpers, unscrupulous coworkers, mob-connected supervisors, and legions of tourists with sawdust for brains and faces of wax. That was the world they shut out once a week in the cabin. Sex was their release. For at least that evening they did not have to worry about diabetes, *plantar fasciitis*, herniated discs, LGLs, triglycerides, or knee replacements they could not afford.

But they all knew they were living on borrowed time. All were in their upper sixties, and none believed they would survive their twilight years with golden parachutes. None of them had relatives with homes where they could room when the moment of retirement came and the thought of living in a single room in a large house with people in the same financial condition as they did not appeal to any of them.

Sadly, their combined debt ceiling was at the level of the bottom of the label of the jar of mayonnaise on the third self of the cabin refrigerator. They, collectively, like Jigger, personally, were caught in the squeeze between rich and poor. They could see the financial opportunities but could not take advantage thereof because they did not have the money to get into the game. Many others in the same circumstances have pooled their moneys and spent the next three decades paying it off. The belief had been—and it was a false belief—that property today would be worth big bucks tomorrow. That might have been true in any city in America—except Las Vegas. The pulsating nature of the real-estate market made any purchase a crapshoot. You could make money. But then, again, you could not. So there the five sat, in a city where money, quite literally, ran down the street, and they could no more predict what was going to happen in the markets in which they were experts than the odds makers in a casino.

Then Zapata discovered she had breast cancer. It was treatable, but the doctor bills were going to be astronomical. Medicare would take a small bite out of the rising mountain of expenses. But only a bite. The next bite would be taken by the cabin.

CHAPTER 23

FOLTZ WANTS A CUT

It took three days for Foltz to pull his head out of his back pocket. For three days he had been spending every spare moment trying to piece together what was happening, what had been happening, over at Peters Title Company. The facts were there—on paper in front of him—but they just did not make sense. He knew that the Rutherford Bank and Trust had given at least eight mortgages to Jean Peters, Dolores Dobbins, Myrrh Frankincense, and Sandoval Wisnoski. The four had then bought and sold more than a dozen properties among themselves. Some of the packages were single homes in foreclosures, while others were odd collections of raw land. Some of the properties were adjacent to each other, while others were blocks away. The only thing they all had in common was that they were in the same section of the city.

What the hell was going on?

Then it hit him.

He had an aha moment sometime between 3:00 a.m. and 5:00 a.m. It was so obvious that it jerked him awake. He had been thinking logically and rationally. He had not been thinking outside of the box. He had been doing exactly what the auditors had been doing. The

136

difference was that the auditors didn't care what was happening as long as no regulations or statutes had been violated. The auditors had found nothing wrong with the transactions because every one of them had been legitimate. It was Immunity by Solidarity. Every transaction had been legal; therefore, no further investigation was necessary. End of story, and the books were closed.

Suddenly he had a very good idea why purchases had been made in late January and early February and more in later April and early May in the previous year. He was willing to bet that the bank auditors for the Rutherford Bank and Trust came sometime in early March. What was happening on the front end was delay. He looked at the documents again. Suddenly things got a little less murky. The mortgage loans were all being filed on different dates. What this meant was that all the paperwork on all the loans were constantly in a state of flux. A bank loan that was given on paper in mid-January would not reach the title company until mid-February. It would eventually clear just as—or just after—the auditors arrived.

So the auditors would not see the mortgages that had just been filed.

The mortgages that had been filed after March of the previous year cleared relatively quickly. Now he was willing to bet that if this process continued, there would be a collection of other mortgages filed the next January and February, this January and February, and delayed just long enough to miss the auditors once again. Sooner or later the auditors were going to catch on to whatever scam was being pulled, but as of this moment, they had not.

But then, again, neither had he.

What the hell was going on here? Money was moving, but no one was making any money?

Then it dawned on him. He was looking at the problem backward!

The key to what was happening was *not who was buying the properties*! It was who was *ending up* with the properties!

137

CHAPTER 24

HAVILL & ELLIOT

Comfort zones are what God gives the lazy to keep the field clear for the ambitious. When it became clear as a Las Vegas evening that Zapata had, at the very least, a financially devastating disease—and quite possibly a life-ending condition—the five friends were forced to move out of their self-imposed comfort zone to see if there was a Plan B for all of them collectively.

Up until that moment, they—individually and collectively—had been content with playing out the poor hand life had dealt them. They lived for their weekly trysts and shut off the consequences of what was reasonably going to happen down the road of life. With blinders, they had purposefully shuttered themselves off from the real world. They had been perfectly happy to remain ignorant. Now the real world had come a-calling. An oncologist had made it clear that their days of benign neglect of the future were over.

Now they were forced to push the envelope.

This was, in itself, not a bad thing. It was a necessary thing, and they, collectively, did what less than 10% of the population could do, would do, had the audacity or intestinal fortitude to do. Anyone can be smart,

138

but it takes real brains to be clever. The world is replete with people who have oceans of knowledge but not a teaspoon of creative thought. But it is those teaspoons of creative thought that move civilization forward. Now that Zapata was facing a crisis, the other five were forced to transition from sedate to clever.

Though not viewed or stated that way, each of the five began plumbing their respective endeavors to see if there was an opportunity for money they had overlooked. The answer was both a yes and a no. Yes, there were opportunities for the bold, but, no, they were not individually or collectively bold enough or rich enough to take advantage of the offering. Besides, the money they needed was *now* money, not *a decade from now* payout.

While there was no Plan B, there was the possibility of a Plan C. As Sherlock Holmes famously stated, once you have eliminated the impossible, whatever remains, however improbable, must be the truth. So the quintuplet stirred the business embers of Las Vegas to see what might flare to life. There was not much, because, after all, there was a very real reason that these business opportunities were in the dying embers, as there was not a dime in any of them.

The only option that was still on the table with no takers was a low-ball offer from a large residential construction company in Minneapolis, Havill & Elliot, which was kind of, sort of, off-and-on interested in expanding into the Las Vegas market. It was interested in buying the equivalent of six city blocks for a residential project. By Las Vegas standards, this was small, only about 30 acres. It could have been a lucrative sale. While the size was enough to interest many Las Vegas Realtors, the offering price was so low that it had been rejected as ridiculous. The corporation offered a lump sum of $60 million for land that, even raw without being on the power and water/sewer grids, was worth beyond $75 million. There had been some weak swats at the offer, but no Realtor was looking at it seriously.

Hopeful that the corporation had come to its senses with regard to Las Vegas real estate, the quintuplet decided to take a swat. So as not to arouse suspicion and generate competition, Bullet made the call. Yes, the corporation told him, they were still interested in coming to Las Vegas, but, no, the $60 million was firm.

The next question was a typical real-estate question. Where did they want the land to be located? Or, more accurately, what would squelch the deal? The response was heartening. The land had to be reasonably close to a thoroughfare, and it had to have city water and sewer reasonably accessible along with power lines. More importantly, it had to be at least 75% title-free—as long as the remaining 25% of the land had homes and very small stores. No malls or casinos, just homes. Or condos.

Then, being a man of the hard-dollar world, Bullet asked a banker's question: was this sale going to be a cash sale? The answer was yes. If the corporation could get the land for $60 million, they would pay cash.

While this answer meant little to Bullet, it did ring a distant bell with Jigger. At the same time Bullet was making his call, the state banking auditors who were then doing their annual cursory look over the mortgage records of Rutherford Bank and Trust had made an odd request. They had asked Jigger to begin arranging the Mortgages of Reconveyance by name, not date. Why, he did not know, but that had been the request.

Being a man of a curious nature, Jigger had wondered why. Mortgage of Reconveyance were records of mortgages that were paid off by the homeowner or subsumed by another mortgage company. This was done all the time and meant very little to Rutherford Bank and Trust. The banks' business—and the mortgage banking business in general—was a pass-through operation. Joe and Jean Smith would want to buy a home. They would fill out the paperwork at Rutherford Bank and Trust and the request for the $500,000. The couple would get the loan and make payments for 20 years, and then the home would be theirs.

Except that most people never paid off their loans. They lived in a house for ten years, sold it, took the equity they had built up over the decade, and dropped it into a new home. Then they started the loan process over again.

With regard to the nuts-and-bolts, when Joe and Jean bought the home, they were given a mortgage. When they sold the home and bought another one, they were, in essence, conducting three real-estate transactions at the same time. First, they were getting a new mortgage via the financial chain of banks from Fannie Mae or Freddie Mac for the new home—say, $700,000. Second, they would sell their home they were living in for its current assessed value of $700,000 and pay off their old mortgage—say, $300,000. Third, they would transfer the remaining $400,000 as a down payment for the new home. Thus, they had jiggled themselves into a $700,000 new home with a $400,000 down payment from the equity in their old home. The couple was happy because now they had a new home with a low monthly mortgage payment because they were able to roll the equity from their old home into their new mortgage. The bank that received the buyou was not happy because someone else was going to buy the $600,000 home so that the monthly interest payments would continue. The bank holding the new mortgage document was happy because now the couple was paying them a monthly mortgage payment. Two Realtors were happy because two homes had been sold—with a 6% fee for each home—and the title companies were happy because two titles had to be transferred.

So what was the big deal with the Mortgages of Reconveyance? he casually asked around.

He got nothing.

Then he casually asked a regulator and got a strange answer. It has something to do with Alaska.

Alaska?

What did the land to polar bears, igloos, and walrus have to do with Las Vegas?

That was a good question.

It was such a good question that he did not have an answer.

But he didn't know anyone in Alaska he could ask.

But Zapata did.

That was because title companies handle interstate documents all the time. Over the years, Zapata had handled paperwork from every state, just like every other title company in America. So she picked up the phone and placed a call to an Alaskan title company. What she got was bits and pieces that made half-sense to her. When she told Jigger, he was able to flesh out the scenario.

It was a peach.

CHAPTER 25

HAROLD CHARLES DOBBINS IN FEDERAL COURT

If Harold Dobbins thought that his appearance in Nevada State Court was a travesty, he likened his appearance in federal court to a three-ring circus. It might not have been so bad if he had been handcuffed and then taken out the back door of the Nevada state court and transferred to federal court in an unmarked vehicle.

But he wasn't.

He was marched out the back door of the courtroom, down three flights of stairs and then back into the mezzanine and out through the front door of the Las Vegas City courthouse toward a taxi in front of the building.

A taxi?

In front of the courthouse?

This **was** a Mickey Mouse operation. Here was the United States Attorney marching a prisoner in handcuffs in a MWLVPD jumpsuit walking out the *front door* of the state of Nevada courthouse and then taking a taxi to the federal courthouse. The only thing Dobbins could think of was that the feds wanted the maximum newspaper publicity they could get.

They got it.

Harold and his escort were mobbed on the sidewalk. There were so many cameras flashing his eyes that he had sunspots. Once into the cab, he was whisked a score of blocks to the federal courthouse and then—once again on the sidewalk—he was taken in the front door of the federal courthouse and led through the lobby and up a public staircase and then into a courtroom on the third floor, cameras flashing and reporters yelling questions the whole way.

There was not going to be any waiting around for the federal judge. She was standing behind her desk when Dobbins came into the courtroom—through the door for spectators. In went Dobbins, and close behind him came the convoy of newspapers and television reporters like a serpentine tail. While the bailiff was yelling for order and for the cameras to be put away, Dobbins was hustled through the gate in the thigh-high trellis that divided the visitors' seating from the Defense and Prosecution tables. Still handcuffed, Harold was stuffed into a wooden chair stage left.

The judge banged the gavel several times and demanded silence. Then she made it clear that if there was any disturbance at all from the seating gallery—and that included photographs being taken—she would clear the room. There was some mumbling and complaining, but when the judge banged her gavel again, the room went silent.

"Well, we are quite the circus here today, Mr. Dobbins."

Harold did not know what to say, so he said nothing.

The judge tilted her glasses on the brow of her nose and looked at a paper she was holding. There was silence for a moment and then she asked for someone from the United States Attorney's office to come to the podium. The white-haired man who had jack-in-the-boxed in state court fought his way through the crowd and the trellis to the podium. He was followed by the three mousey IRS agents.

"Do I read this correctly?" The judge removed her glasses and pointed an earpiece at the attorney. "You are asking that Mr. Dobbins be held as a material witness because he allegedly received fifty million dollars from a woman who is not the first wife of Howard Hughes and to whom Howard Hughes for some reason allegedly left fifty million dollars. Is this correct?"

"Yes, your honor. The IRS . . ."

"That's fine, counselor. I will ask the IRS agents who, I presume, are seated at the Prosecutor Table."

"Yes, your honor, it is their case. We, the United States Attorney's office, that is, are here as a courtesy to the IRS. They prevailed upon us to . . ."

"I figured that out on my own, counselor. You can be seated." As the attorney found his seat, Titterington house jack-rabbited up.

"And you are?" asked the judge.

"I am Special Agent Jane Titterington with the IRS."

"OK. What's going on?"

"Your honor, several days ago, the IRS received a copy of a codicil allegedly signed by Howard Hughes giving one Jean Peters fifty million dollars."

"Jean Peters being the first wife of Howard Hughes."

"That's what we assume, your honor. The Jean Peters who should have received the codicil was the first wife of Howard Hughes. But she died in 2000. This codicil was given to another Jean Peters."

"How do you know the codicil was not destined for the Jean Peters who was not Howard Hughes 'wife?"

"That's not reasonable, your honor."

"Maybe. Maybe not. Did this other Jean Peters have any relationship with Howard Hughes?"

"Not that we know of."

"OK. If this other Jean Peters received the codicil, why is Mr. Dobbins in court?"

"Because we cannot find the other Jean Peters. She is missing."

"Missing as in dead?"

"No, your honor. She is missing as in we cannot locate her. We know she bought a ticket to Manilla last week, and there the trail ends."

145

"So she is in the Philippines?"

"We don't know."

"And you don't know if she is coming back?"

"That is correct, your honor."

"Again, why is Mr. Dobbins in my courtroom?"

"Our information and documentation indicate that Mr. Dobbins is to receive Jean Peters's estate in the event of her death."

"But she's not dead."

"Not as far as we know."

"I am confused. This Jean Peters is not dead as far as you know, but you are holding Mr. Dobbins as a material witness because he is in a will of a woman who has yet to die. Is that correct?"

"Yes, your honor. We have credible evidence to believe that Mr. Dobbins has already hidden the fifty million dollars Jean Peters received from the Howard Hughes codicil."

"How do you know that?"

"We have checked Jean Peters's financial history, and she does not have fifty million dollars. We have checked Mr. Dobbin's financial records and history, and he does not have fifty million dollars. Further, we cannot find any corporations, shell company, or investment portfolio anywhere in the United States in which either person has an interest. Our auditors are diligent, your honor, and we have asked both state and federal bank auditors to assist us. They are doing so as we speak."

"You have bank auditors looking for the money? Aren't bank auditors supposed to be overlooking banking practices?"

"Yes, your honor. But fifty million dollars is a substantial amount."

"So instead of auditing banks, they are looking for money that may or may not exist?"

"We believe it exists. Or it did exist and is now hidden."

"I want to make sure that I understand what you are saying. You are saying that Jean Peters and Mr. Dobbins must have fifty million dollars because you have not found it?"

"Yes, your honor."

"And you want Mr. Dobbins held until you can find the money?"

"Yes, your honor."

"If it exists are all?"

"Yes, your honor."

"Why? If Jean Peters is still alive, there can be no inheritance. No inheritance means that Mr. Dobbins cannot get the fifty million dollars even if he knows where it is, even if he has hidden it."

"Mr. Dobbins is a flight risk. He can take the fifty million dollars and flee the country."

"But how do you know that there is fifty million dollars to find? Do you have the codicil?"

"We have a photocopy of the codicil but not the original document."

"Where did you get the photocopy?"

"From a reliable source."

"But it has not been authenticated?"

"That cannot happen until we get the original."

"Where is the original?"

"In Jean Peter's safety deposit box."

"You know that for a fact?"

"Our source tells us the codicil is there, as well as a will from Jean Peters leaving Mr. Dobbins her estate, which we believe includes the fifty million dollars."

"Where is Jean Peters's safety deposit box?"

"Rutherford Bank and Trust, a small bank here in town. We have identified the box number."

"Let me guess. You want this court to hold Mr. Dobbins as a material witness until the safety box of Jean Peters is opened and the codicil is authenticated."

"Yes, your honor."

"I am going to make a wild guess and suggest you want me to issue a warrant to open Jean Peters's safety deposit box to retrieve the codicil."

"That is correct, your honor."

"What happens if the codicil is not there?"

"We believe it is there. If it is not, there is no reason for Mr. Dobbins to be held."

"If the codicil is not there, will you continue to look for the fifty million dollars?"

"The IRS is vigilant, your honor. We will attempt to backtrack the money."

"I see. I find it hard to justify keeping Mr. Dobbins in custody on the basis of your word that an unnamed informant provided your office with a photocopy of a document that cannot be verified, alleging fifty million dollars, that may or may not exist, left by a man dead half a century to a woman he may have confused with his first wife because both had the same name. Do I have this right?"

"Well, yes, your honor. But the proof is in the document. Once Jean Peters's safety deposit box is opened—"

"With my warrant."

"Yes, your honor. With your warrant. Once the safety deposit box is opened, we will be able to determine our next step."

"No. If I authorize the opening of the safety deposit box, and the codicil is not there, this will end the harassment of Mr. Dobbins. Is that clear?"

"Well, your honor, there is the matter of authentication."

"That goes without saying. If the codicil is not there, this case is defunct." The judge looked hard at Titterington. "Defunct as in history, as in yesterday's stock market numbers."

"Yes, your honor."

"If the codicil is found and is not one hundred percent authenticated, this matter is also defunct, doornail dead. Is that clear?"

"Well, your honor, no one can get a one hundred percent authentication."

"Well, it had better be statistically close to one hundred percent if this case comes back to my court." She paused for a moment and then said, "And it will come back to this court. Once the safety deposit box is opened, how long will it take to authenticate the codicil?"

"Well, it could take months, your honor."

"No, it will take no longer than five days. By this Friday."

"Your honor!"

"Five days. I will hold Mr. Dobbins no longer than five days, which, as far as I am concerned, is five days longer than he should be held on such a wild-goose chase." The judge shook the paper she was holding. "And Mr. Dobbins will not be held in a federal jail. He will be placed in more luxurious quarters and the bill passed along to your department."

Titterington tried to object, but she was too late.

"This case is in recess until nine a.m. Friday."

Her gavel came down.

CHAPTER 26

ASSUMPTIONS AND PERCEPTIONS ARE YOUR ENEMY

Prof started Wednesday's class with a story. He told of a young man and young woman in the days before the Internet. They had never met each other, but they had been introduced via snail mail by mutual friends. They corresponded as pen pals and decided to get married. Neither had seen pictures of the other. On the day of the wedding, the groom was delayed at the airport and barely made it to the church on time. He rushed into the wedding and saw the bride for the first time.

She was black.

Prof stalled for a moment, and there was a low-level groan in the classroom. There were a couple of *ouches* and *ohss* and then Prof said the problem here was not the story or some students' reactions. "The problem here—and the real-life problem—is that you are letting your perceptions and assumptions get in the way of what is really important. You don't know if the groom was black. You don't know if the groom was white and didn't care that the bride was black. In fact, all you know for sure is that the bride was black."

Prof continued, "Perhaps the single most important lesson for you to learn in life is to learn to think outside of the box. In life, ninety-five percent of the difficulties you will face can be solved logically and rationally. That's why they are called difficulties and not problems. Problems cannot be solved with logical, rational thinking. If they could, they would be difficulties and solved. But it is those five percent that will determine the course of your life.

"Thinking outside of the box is difficult because the logical rational approach has been drummed into your head since you were a child. Allow me to give you a few adages, and see, if you can, the fallacy of the statements. How about 'you cannot teach an old dog new tricks.' Anyone who has ever had a dog knows this to be inaccurate. You cannot teach a stupid dog a new trick because the stupid dog never learned one trick to begin with. 'A stitch in time saves nine,' if you are going to keep the shirt. But if the shirt is a T-shirt, it's not worth your time to stitch it up. One of my favorite nonsense adages that is truly misleading is that the early bird gets the worm and the second mouse gets the cheese. Birds get worms all day long, and a smart mouse gets the cheese without caught.

"This lesson is extremely important to everyone in this class," Prof said, "because, whether you know it or not, you are being educated for jobs that do not yet exist. No one knows where technological advances will carry us over the next four years. Creative thinking prepares you for jobs that do not yet exist. You have to learn to think outside the box to be able to take advantage of the opportunities coming your way."

He continued, saying, "Many of the students believe that if you work hard, you can maneuver yourself into the right place at the right time. Maybe. Maybe not. But you have to be prepared for the moment you are in the right place at the right time. That's why you have to learn to think outside of the box. Just as important, you cannot let your perception and assumptions get in the way of understanding what is really happening. If you do, you've been snookered—and you can look up that term in Wikipedia.

"What is going on with the Hughes codicil is an excellent example of letting your perceptions and assumptions run wild," he said. "This week has been an absolute circus with the IRS, SEC, Las Vegas Police Department, state court, federal court, newspapers, television stations, and now the state of Nevada Gaming Control Board. It has been absolute chaos. But it is organized chaos."

At this point Prof passed out a color copy of the Egyptian god, Seth. "Oddly," Prof stated, "Seth is the most identifiable of all Egyptian gods but the most misunderstood. He is a man with straight black hair that hangs to the middle of his chest. He has the face of an anteater with ears like a rabbit but are squared on top. Seth is singular because he is the god of organized chaos, a concept those who think logically and rationally cannot fathom. 'Organized chaos' is a *non-sequitur*, an oxymoron. If something is organized, there is no chaos. If there is chaos, by the very definition of the word, it is not organized. So what is 'organized chaos,' and why did the Greeks have such a hard time transubstantiating it into their philosophy that, by extension, is ours?

"Organized chaos?

"OK, how about an example?

"Let's leap forward to our time. Have you ever worked for a large organization? It doesn't make any difference what the organization does. It could be a television station, government office, hospital, or even a factory that makes cast-iron piggy banks. It doesn't make any difference what job you did either. All that does matter is what you saw happening at work. In all likelihood you came home on more than one occasion actually amazed that anything got done at all. One-third of the employees were either incompetent or asleep at the switch. There were people who came in late and employees who left early. People used sick leave as soon as they got it. Quality control went to hell in a hand basket as soon as the supervisor turned his back, and at every meeting the sales manager talked about how no one was meeting quotas. The incoming raw material was substandard, the marketing staff had no idea what they were doing, and the only time you ever saw the president of the corporation was on a video conference where you sat in a room with two hundred other people. Of the six people with whom you worked most closely, two were idiots and one 'had an agenda' you do not understand to this day. You would die rather than have a beer with ninety-seven percent of the people who worked there, and if it wasn't for the paycheck, frankly, you'd have been gone within a few weeks of being on the job. So you did what everyone else does: put in your time, hoping to get a large enough saving to retire before the organization went under.

"Sounds familiar.

"Further, if you talked to someone five years after you've left that job, you would find that nothing would have changed. The organization would still be a mess, even after all the innovative management techniques, fresh blood, new equipment, 'better' software, and getting rid of deadwood.

"Whatever new job you get, it will be the same old, same old. Whether you are in the military, work for the federal government, put your time in with the state, put up with the municipal bureaucracy, run the rat race in the private sector, or slog it out in a nonprofit, it's all the same. Bigger is not always better and never very efficient.

"That's organized chaos.

"In reality there is so much organized chaos in our world that it is amazing that we remain sane. No matter where you live in the world, the traffic is bad. *Very* bad. It could be a lot better if everyone followed the rules of the road, but you know how that is. 'Rules?' people snap. 'I don't need no stinkin' rules!' These are the kind of people who get a reckless driving ticket and *swear* that this was the *first* time they had ever weaved through fifty-miles-per-hour traffic at seventy miles per hour in a forty-five-miles-per-hour zone, and why wasn't everyone *else* being given a ticket for going too fast anyway? Every country in the world has a crime rate that would be a lot worse if it was not for the cops. Every capitol in the world has corruption. Every city in the world has pollution. Every neighborhood has a pedophile and every home a sinner. We need the government and the police and the newspapers and the churches just to keep societies in check. If the forces of organization weren't in operation all the time, our world would be one of unrestrained chaos instead of organized chaos.

"That's organized chaos.

"The reason few people know about Seth today was because the Greeks, philosophically, killed him. That's because the world of Greeks—which we inherited—was a place where perfection and harmony could be reached in human life. That is, there was a universal law into which all things fit, and that world could be adjusted to be perfect. For example, the Greeks knew that there was universality to mathematics. One and one was two wherever in the world one happened to be. They also knew when the weather got cold, water would become ice. They could predict the path of the sun, moon, planets, and stars in the heavens and understand the cycle of life. This led them to the belief that the world was not a collection of grubby people scratching out a living on the hillsides of every country but part of a grand scheme that had universal rules.

"The key to a productive life is to know what is important and, using a sports expression, 'keep your eye on the ball.' Ninety percent of your life will be wasted; it's the other ten percent that counts. Continuing the sport metaphor, consider a football game. In the entire four quarters—all of one hundred twenty minutes, which include time-outs, advertising, and delays because of penalties—there are only about eleven minutes when the ball is actually in play. Eleven minutes, about ten percent of the time. If you play Defense, you can cut that time by half. With Special Teams, you can drop it by half again. The rest of the game all the teams are doing is killing grass.

"But you have to play the whole game, from starting kickoff until the gun goes off one hundred twenty minutes later.

"Now, mixing in Aristotle and Plato, the two philosophers might say that the embodiment of their principles can be seen in those eleven minutes. It will be a mixture of faith and reason and one's best chance of leaving the game a complete person—win or lose—would be to keep the faith and read the other guy's plays. Everything else is just muscle and sweat and luck.

"On the other hand, were Seth to watch a football game, he would have been elated. He would see himself personified on the field. At the beginning of each play, both sides know what they are supposed to do. They have planned it. They line up in precise order and then, when the ball is snapped, anything can happen. It is organized chaos. Scholars rumble with the street folk, and even the biggest of players can be brought low by the smallest of physiques. There are so many factors involved that on any Sunday, any football team can beat any other team regardless of how the bookies in Las Vegas call the spread.

"What's the point here?

"What does any of this have to do with the Hughes codicil? Well," Prof stated, "there is one helluva lot of organized chaos around the codicil. Every possible agency is involved. Ninety percent of what is happening is wasted effort. We know that. That's life. What we do not know is where the true ten percent of quality activity is. We know that something is happening, but we—and the alphabet soup of state and federal agencies—do not know what it is. At some point in history we will know, but right now there is utter chaos in Las Vegas.

"Next week could be the most important week in your educational life," he continued. "You are watching some very clever people creating chaos for reasons only they know. See if you can figure out what is happening. Write it down because by this time next week, it will all be over. Don't let your assumptions and perceptions get in the way. See if you can be as clever as those people who have set Seth loose in this modern age. As I keep telling you"—and the class spoke along with Prof—"history is not the story of the past; it is the study of the future."

155

CHAPTER 27

FOLTZ CUTS IN

Long before the sun came up, Foltz was on his computer. The state of Nevada land records were online, and he punched up one of the properties at random. Then he followed the sale from Peters to Dobbins to Frankincense to Wisnoski. In the past he had stopped there. Now he took the next step. What happened to the property after the sale to Sandoval Wisnoski?

Bingo!

The property was transferred to Juggernaut, Inc. of Los Angeles. Foltz then pulled up the other properties and followed their peripatetic transactional trail, and they too—all of them—ended up in Juggernaut, Inc. of Los Angeles.

Who was Juggernaut, Inc. of Los Angeles?

Foltz did not know, but the state of California web page let him pull up the corporate paperwork. Juggernaut, Inc. of Los Angeles had been formed the previous January and was one person: Jeremy Mooney with a post-office box in Las Vegas.

Jigger!

Foltz knew Jigger. They had both gone to junior college in banking years ago. The old, fat black guy in the classes. Jeremy Mooney! That's right. So that was the scam! Mooney was laundering money for the bank! Or was he? Looking through the paperwork, he realized that, in fact, Rutherford Bank and Trust was *not* actually making money on the sales!

If that was the case, what the hell was going on? It couldn't be that complicated if a black guy like Mooney was involved. He had to be fronting for someone else. After all, a *black* guy orchestrating something this sophisticated? Come on!

CHAPTER 28

THE PLAN IS HATCHED

"God, in his infinite wisdom—" started Jigger, but Myrrh cut him off.

"*Her* infinite wisdom," she said.

"Whatever," Jigger continued. "His, her, or its infinite wisdom works in mysterious ways. There is an opportunity for all of us here, but it has a lot of moving parts. There's also a final wrap-up sort of requirement. By that I mean what I am going to propose is going to attract a lot of attention with the IRS and regulators. The good news is, if we hit it right, we'll walk away with about ten million dollars cash each, all legal and tax-free."

He paused for effect and then said, "Maybe."

He paused for effect again. "If I want to pay taxes. Paying off a mortgage is paying off a debt. There is no income. So there might not be any taxes due. But . . ."

Again, he paused for effect and then said, "That could change at any moment. I don't trust the IRS or the state banking regulators or the SEC or any of the other federal banking geeks. I've been dealing with them for too long. They don't care when you don't have money. Then, when you do, they can find all kinds *of* parenthetical clauses that end up costing you money. As soon as the IRS and the SEC figure out what we are doing, they are going to change the rules. Possibly retroactively. They can do that, you know.

"So, when I say this is an end-of-story, EOS, sort of opportunity, I am saying that I, for one, am going to be leaving the country. I'll get my money, pay my taxes without the ten million dollar gift mortgage, and then I and my money are going to the Bahamas. If the alphabet soup of federals want to try to get my money, I'm not reachable. If they change the rules, I don't come back to the United States, so I won't have to face audits and awkward questions."

The other four looked at him oddly.

They were silent.

"Let me get this right," Dolores said as she shook her head in jerks. "What you are saying is that we've got a chance to end up with $10 million apiece and pay no taxes on it?"

Jigger nodded. "Yes. But we have to do it right. We have to make sure every single thing we do is perfect." He spelled the word out. "P-e-r-f-e-c-t. A little luck won't hurt, but I think I've got the details worked out pretty well. Every one of us will have a critical role to play, and none of us, not one of us, can fall down on the job. We are going to be running on the ragged edge. Like I said, the instant this finishes, we've got to get gone. All of us. What we are doing is legal, in the sense that we are not breaking any laws, *b-u-t* we will be slamming up against some regulatory walls. It will take the regulators a while to put together what we did, but by then we have to be out of the country."

"I don't have any problem leaving the United States," Bullet cut in. "I sure don't have any problem living in Bahamas. Can we all go together?"

"It doesn't matter how we go or where we go," Jigger said. "I'm just saying that to be safe, we have to leave the jurisdiction of the United States and leave behind nothing but dust. I'd like to think we'll all go together. We have a great little group here, and there's a lot of satisfaction. We're all pushing seventy, which means we've only got another ten years of joy before the bad joints and cholesterol move in big-time. I'd rather not spend five years trying to find another group that shares as much joy as we have now. Yes, I think we should all go together. I'm just saying it is my recommendation that we complete this operation and be gone. Long gone by the time the regulators pull everything together."

"How much time do we have?" Zapata pulled out a calendar.

"Here's how I figure it. This entire operation is going to take three major efforts. Cleverly done and scrambling of the paperwork, we can have two of those efforts completed before anyone can figure out what we are going. But then we are going to have to have a distraction. Realtors are not stupid. They are going to catch on to what we are doing. So are the regulators. We also have to assume that some clever freelancers will catch up to us before we can leave town. We just have to move faster than all of them can. We can do that because we know what we are doing; they don't. If we can come up with a good way to stall them, we should be able to pull this off and be out of the country with ten-million-dollar tax-free money in the Bahamas."

"How do we start?" asked Myrrh.

Jigger smiled. "I'm glad you asked."

CHAPTER 29

JIGGER GETS A VISIT

Reginal Rutherford did not look anything like a president and chief financial officer of a bank. Any bank. He looked like a string bean with a toupee. He topped six foot seven, had never played basketball, sported kneecaps so large they stretched his trouser legs, and had feet so small he had to buy women's shoes.

His appearance was misleading. When it came to business, he was sharp as a tack. He had a business degree from UCLA, MBA from USC, and had spent five years with the accounting giant Ernst & Ernst before it had been swallowed by another accounting whale. He started his own hole-in-the-wall quick loan office that grew into a modestly large bank in Las Vegas because he was willing to take risks other bankers shied away from considering. He knew what was what. On the other hand, he had never been guilty of having a single original thought.

Of great importance in the banking game, he was adept at seeing miniscule problems on the horizon that could get very large very fast. It took him until May to get around to reading the bank audit of the previous March. Once again, Rutherford Bank and Trust had been given a clean bill of health. But in the appendix of the audit where the

161

percentages were listed, he noticed an aberration, an increase in bad debt. The amount was not numerically significant when compared to the net assets of the bank, but it was statistically significant when compared with previous years.

More important, the total amount was edging toward audit radar range. Bad debt was both a concerning fact of banking vitality while, at the same time, a necessary part of banking life. Banking losses reduced banking profits, which, in turn, reduced the corporate income tax. The important real-life concern of a bank was that its bad debts were an actuarial sleight of hand and not a hard-dollar loss.

Rutherford had two combined concerns. Was the bad debt going to rise above the audit radar in the next quarter? If it did, it could trigger an intensive audit of the bank's books. Even though Rutherford Bank and Trust had nothing big to hide, SEC and FDIC auditors did not spend months going over a bank' records and find nothing. Every bank had something to hide. The larger the bank, the larger the secrets. Federal auditors liked plumbing bank records, and the bigger the bank the better. If they had to look, they would find something. So, to keep the auditors away, banks kept their accounting categories below specific percentages. This was colloquially known as radar range. As long as your accounting categories were below radar range, the federal auditors left the bank alone.

But, speaking internally, something was afoot. Bank executives across the country were keenly aware of the gift mortgage problem in Alaska, and every banker from San Diego to Bar Harbor wanted to make sure that the gift-mortgage investigation stopped in Alaska. Every bank from San Diego to Bar Harbor was gifting mortgages, just not the extent that Alaskan banks were.

Every bank was concerned.

But not too concerned. The basic problem in Alaska was as old as humanity: greed. The banks in Alaska pushed over radar range, and the auditors came in big-time.

Gift mortgages were a time-honored practice. It was basically giving people free money from the bank. But the money was not free. In reality, it was federal money, taxpayer money, the reason that federal auditors were involved. A bank would give a deserving soul a mortgage and then, a week later, pay off the loan with a Mortgage of Reconveyance. The deserving soul would then get a free house. Since the individual had not paid off the house with cash, the bank could not have received payment for the mortgage. The bank listed the gifted mortgage as a bad debt. Banks could do this because financial transactions are legally viewed as consummated when the paperwork closes. In legalese, this means that the initial mortgage transaction starts with the request for mortgage money by the bank and ends with the borrower signing the mortgage document. When the lender pays off the mortgage—or the mortgage is paid off by the bank—a new financial transaction is originated. From the auditor's point of view, these are two independent financial transactions that are mutually exclusive. Auditing standards require auditors to evaluate financial transactions in the singular, not sequentially. This frees the bank to give "deserving souls" free homes.

What made gift mortgages so financially delicious was that the money for the mortgage was federal money. It was not the bank's money. But in the Morphean universe, it was the bank's money and could be listed as a bad debit that reduced the bank's corporate income tax obligation.

The news for the "deserving souls" got even better. A mortgage is a debt. Paying off a debt does not generate income. It is just paying off a debt. If someone pays off a credit card balance of $1,000, the person does not have to list the $1,000 as income. Thus, the $400,000 mortgage that is gifted is not income. No income means no income tax. It's free money.

The problem in Alaska was that one particular bank kept giving a lot of "deserving souls" a lot of gift mortgages. In some cases, the bank kept giving the same "deserving souls" three, four, or even five gift mortgages for the same house over a very short period of time. Upward of $150 million in gift mortgages had been given out over a five-year period. That, in itself, had not been enough to spark the audit. The bank in question was very large, and the $150 million scattered over multiple years did not raise the interest of the SEC or the FDIC.

What did cause a problem was the discovery of who was getting the gift mortgages.

A local historian looking at land records found that gift mortgages in sequence were being given to state representatives, judges, police chiefs, mayors, municipal attorneys, the governor, and two attorney generals. The historian reasoned that the SEC must have known about the gift mortgages because the bank was audited regularly. Since the practice was ongoing, he reported the gifting to the United States Department of Justice Office of Public Integrity. What the historian had unexpectedly done was protest the gift mortgages outside of the chain of financial command of those who knew and tacitly approved of the process. Had the protest been sent to the SEC, nothing would have happened.

But the protest was not initially sent to the SEC.

It was sent to the Office of Public Integrity in the Justice Department.

The Office of Public Integrity had never heard of gift mortgages. Now that it had, a Department of Justice investigation was opened, and the entire can of worms was spilled onto the judicial table. It suddenly became a big problem because the Department of Justice was looking at the practice as being felonious, not just an accounting issue. Felonious meant jail time, not the proverbial slap on the fiduciary wrist and a warning not to do it again.

It did not take long for the word to filter down to all banks in America that gift mortgages were under scrutiny. But, again, as long as the transactions were few and of low amounts, the auditors were likely to wink them away. No bank wanted to be audited for something as usual as a gift mortgage, so all bank CFOs began taking a hard look at the Bad Debt category because that was where the telltale trail of the gift mortgage was likely to be discovered.

It was that reason that Rutherford called Jigger into his office.

This being said, banking conversations, it is critical to note, do not meet the communication standards in other industries. In carpentry, as an example, when two carpenters have an occupational conversation, high-quality information is exchanged. This could include the precise measurement of a cabinet, the size of nails to use on the support two-by-fours, possible rain damage by installing the cabinets before the roof was completed, or the age of the building contractor because the style of cabinets was switched and the *wrong* cabinets had been installed in the correct space.

By comparison, banking conversations are obtuse. The point is *not* to pass along pertinent information. The overall structure of the exchange is to make sure the CFO has just enough information from documents that are public knowledge to sleep soundly but not enough arcane knowledge that he would fail a lie-detector test.

After perfunctory remarks, Rutherford noted that over the past 18 months, 11 individuals "seemed to have acquired" mortgage assistance. Those individuals were Jean Peters, J. Peters, Myrrh Frankincense, M. Frankincense, Sandoval Wisnoski, S. Wisnoski, S. J. Wisnoski, Dolores Dobbins, D. Dobbins, Jerome Foltz, and J. Foltz. Collectively, these 11 individuals—and Rutherford accented the word *individuals* because, legally and actuarially speaking, they were 11 separate individuals and not five masqueraders. The total amount of the mortgages was above $30 million, which, Rutherford hinted, was rather extravagant.

This was true, Jigger told Rutherford. But because of the auditing standard that limited information to only the flow of money, *one*—and Jigger used that generic term for a person rather than *you*—could not see the whole picture. The individuals in question were recycling the mortgage money. Individually and collectively, they were getting gift-mortgage moneys that were then used to buy raw land and foreclosed property held by or purchased at a discount by Rutherford Bank and Trust. No actual cash was changing hands. From the point of view of the bank—and not the auditors—the bank was legally recycling money. It was borrowing $500,000 from the mortgage chain of banks and then gift-mortgaging the total amount. This was a bad debt to the bank, which reduced its income tax. In a separate transaction, the $500,000 returned to the bank when it was used to buy raw property or homes in foreclosure owned by the bank. The bank was thus getting its own money back and, at the same time, getting worthless properties off its books. No actual cash was leaving the bank. Everything was a paper transfer. By the end of the process, the bank would have earned no actual money but would have ended up with a tax deduction of $30 million worth of bad debt that would lower its tax obligation while, at the same time, riding itself of foreclosed property that had no current value.

Rutherford took a few minutes to examine the audit report and was pleased—and surprised—to see Jigger was accurate. Even though there had been an elevated increase in the number of properties purchased by the bank, the number of foreclosed properties had gone down substantially. (Why hadn't he noticed that before?)

What Rutherford did not mention was that Jigger only had one mortgage. It was ten years old, and he had been making payments regularly. As long as Jigger did not directly profit from any of the gift-mortgage transactions, what was being done was legal. Rutherford was also smart enough to know that Jigger was going to be making some money somehow, but this he, Rutherford, did not want to know how that was going to occur. He also did not mention it to Jigger.

But what Rutherford did say was what Jigger already knew. "You know," Rutherford said, cautiously choosing his words, "Jerome Foltz is a rather untrustworthy fellow. He's the kind of a person who reads his checkbook for relaxation."

Jigger just smiled.

CHAPTER 30

THE TRAP IS SPRUNG

There is an old adage that if March comes in like a lion, it goes out like a lamb. Or vice versa. Saturday, March 14, was midway between the beginning and end of the month, and regardless of whether the month came in like a lion or a lamb, it was a transitional moment. Both lion and lamb were present in the basement of the federal building that morning. The lion of the combined state and federal government regulators were about to go after a lamb, Harold Dobbins. It was a frenetic scene as men, who had never met each other before, were being welded into a joint state-federal task force to investigate what everyone but the IRS agents felt was as wild a goose chase as there was ever going to be.

But the IRS was calling the shots, and all orders from all state and federal agencies had come from "on high." You did not backtalk "on high."

The IRS took the stage first.

"OK, listen up, folks. For those of you who do not know me, I am Special IRS Agent Jane Titterington. Some of you have worked together before but, for the record, let me give an overview to make sure we are all reading from the same sheet of music. If I say anything that contradicts what you have been told in your respective offices, I, we, the IRS, want to know it now. There is no one person or agency in charge here. There are a lot of moving parts here, and we have to make sure we cover all our basis.

"I, of course, am with the IRS, and we've heard all the IRS jokes. While we have a sense of humor, we don't think anything is funny. The rumor is that we are heartless beasts. But that's only on a good day. Basically we are called in when the people we are going after are very, very bad and no one in local law enforcement can handle the job. We don't have any politics to worry about. We go in, look at books, and seize assets. When we are called, the situation is really bad.

"We are the lead agency, so to speak. We have been informed through a reliable source there exists a codicil from Howard Hughes, which leaves—rather, left—fifty million dollars to one Jean Peters. We are not sure what to believe at this point. Howard Hughes's first wife was Jean Peters, and she got a very nice settlement from Howard Hughes when they were divorced in 1971. It is reasonably possible that the codicil in question—which we believe is dated in 1971—is authentic but that it went to the wrong Jean Peters. Thus, when it comes to the codicil itself, we have to determine if it is authentic, if the money went to the wrong Jean Peters, and, if these two items are correct, what happened to the fifty million dollars mentioned in the codicil.

"Nothing happened with regard to Mr. Dobbins until last year. Then three things happened at once. Mr. Dobbins lost his job at the Cypress Casino and got a part-time job at Peters Title Company. Then the buying of large number of low-value lots started. We do not believe it is a coincidence that Dobbins started working for a title company and soon thereafter millions in real-estate transactions occurred. We suspect that Mr. Dobbins, Jean Peters, and the other employees at Peters Title Company are converting the fifty million dollars into real estate. As you know, we have seized Mr. Dobbins as a material witness and a flight risk. We cannot charge him with anything—yet—and cannot do so until we authenticate the codicil. The codicil is in the safety box of Jean Peters at the Rutherford Bank and Trust, and Jean Peters is in the wind, the Philippines, so we will need court order to open the safety deposit box. The IRS will hold Mr. Dobbins as a material witness until we retrieve the codicil and have an expert examine it. Once the codicil has been authenticated, we will follow the money trail through the Peters Title Company. That is going to be fairly easy because all the real-estate titles have been put in a shell corporation out of Los Angeles. In the meantime, the state of Nevada Division of Bank Audits will put off its regular audit of the Rutherford Bank and Trust until the Howard Hughes's codicil is authenticated. Harry!"

CHAPTER 31

ID-10-T

Jerry Kemp of the Las Vegas *Polite* Department had a special file for unique individuals. It was labeled ID-10-T, and it contained the nutcases of the department. Whenever someone on the telephone told of Elvis on the spaceship, Kemp got the call. When e-mails of alien landings came in, they were routed to Kemp. Walk-ins with proof of who shot J. R. were directed to Kemp's office as well. He got the full-of-the-moon loonies, survivors of flesh-eating bats, reports of man-eating spiders, giant scorpions on the loose, succubus encounters, JFK conspiracy buffs, and dancing with little green men from flying saucers. He got the calls because he was polite, treated the callers with respect, and dutifully placed his well-written reports in the ID-10-T file.

Everyone at the Las Vegas Police Department, including the chief, was absolutely, positively sure Kemp should have gotten the call from the IRS to pick up Harold Dobbins. The IRS logic was right up there with Kokopelli sightings. Kemp agreed, but there was a very big difference between the usual cases he handled and Dobbins. In the case of Dobbins, the publicity had *preceded* the involvement of the police.

In most cases, whether Kemp was called or the "real" police were involved, the investigation of the matters precipitated the involvement of the press. The police would get a 911 call of a murder in a residence, and by the time the homicide unit arrived at the home, the press was already there. Courtesy of freedom of the airwaves, the press would know what was happening as fast as the cop in the patrol car. The press would cluster around the home on the sidewalk—where it could legally stand and report—and then try for interviews with paramedics, homicide detectives, and neighbors. In 99 cases out of 100, the press got to the crime scene *after* the police had been notified.

In the case of Dobbins, the exact opposite was the case. The Hughes codicil had hit the news media *ahead* of any call to the Las Vegas Police Department. But this was not the only oddity of the case. Under normal circumstances, the Las Vega police would not even have bothered to investigate. Kemp would have logged the call in, did a write-up for the ID-10-T file, and moved on to other matters. There was no crime here. There was not even a misdemeanor here. There was zip. Goose egg. Zilch. *Niento.* Zero.

But the Hughes codicil story did ring some kind of a bell with the IRS. Kemp was sure that some ID-10-T in the upper reaches of the IRS read the story and said to himself—or herself—"We'd better get out in front of this story because it's already in the newspaper." Then he—or she—found a fellow ID-10-T in the bowels of the department and said, "Make a big deal out of this so we look like we are on top of it." That agent at the bottom either could not find a federal judge who looked at the case without breaking into hysterical laugher or she—in this case it was her, Agent Titterington—didn't try. She just went to the Las Vegas Police Department as an interdepartmental favor. The request had been made on a Sunday when the officer in charge could not get a no from the top brass because he could not reach them at 7:00 a.m. More likely, Kemp thought, who would want to wake up the chief of police to approve a bona fide request from a federal agency even if was a wild hair? It was a nothing call, a courtesy.

171

A courtesy it may have been, but by the time the Las Vegas police had picked up Dobbins, it was a full-blown publicity disaster. The press was seven leagues ahead of the police by the time Dobbins was in the back of the patrol car. The sidewalk around the station was chockablock with television cameras when Dobbins arrived at the station—at 7:00 a.m.! Suddenly that courtesy had turned into a full-blown disaster.

The only saving grace was that the Las Vegas Police Department had washed its hands off the publicity disaster.

Until late Wednesday afternoon.

Kemp picked up the call from the last person on earth he or, for that matter, anyone in the Las Vegas Police Department wanted to speak with: Walter Otterburg, publisher/editor/reporter for *Las Vegas Scandal, Inc.* Otterburg wanted to know if it was true that Jerome Foltz, well-known Las Vegas bottom-feeder and casino slime ball (Otterburg's description of Foltz, off the record, matched that of Kemp and everyone in the Las Vegas Police Department.), was conspiring with the half brother of the late and not lamented Anthony "Tony the Ant" Spilotro to establish a casino in Las Vegas with mob money from the East Coast.

Kemp said he doubted it.

"Yeah," replied Otterburg and proceeded to inform Kemp that Foltz was a 100% owner of a shell company in California, which was named Acme, which had picked up—*for free!*—six pieces of property in six different blocks in downtown Las Vegas within two blocks from the Strip, which were individually owned by three casinos and three hotels.

Worse, Otterburg had copies of the titles to the six pieces of property.

Did the Las Vegas Police Department care to comment for *Las Vegas Scandal, Inc.*?

172

CHAPTER 32

THE PLOT IS THINNED OUT

The auditor for the state of Nevada, who looked like Clark Gable but with white hair, took the microphone.

"For those of you who don't know me, I'm Harry Dunbar. I've been an auditor for the SEC since before some of you were born."

There was some laughter, and someone in the room yelled, "Here! Here!"

"Unlike the IRS, I'll start with a joke. Whenever my wife has a hard time sleeping, I tell her about my work. That puts her to sleep right away."

There were some titters.

"I'm going to take a few moments of your time to give you an overview of what has been happening. Nothing out of the ordinary was happening between the Rutherford Bank and Trust and Peters Title Company until shortly after Mr. Dobbins was fired from Cypress Casino. Cypress Casino has had more than its fair share of problems with the Nevada Gaming Control Board, but today, as far as the board is concerned, neither Rutherford nor Peters companies have given us any problems. Rather, let me restate that, there was nothing of significance to report other than the usual suspicious mortgages. Because of the gift-mortgage frauds in Alaska, we will be looking at the mortgages differently this year, but, until this year there was nothing out of whack with regard to the mortgage transfers. But as soon as Dobbins—that is, Mr. Dobbins because his aunt, Dolores Dobbins, also works for Peters Title Company—became employed, things began to get odd. You put that map up on the screen, Diane?"

Everyone looked as a map popped onto the screen at the front of the room.

"OK," Harry continued, "here's what we have. Five individuals have been playing fast and loose with gift mortgages. Clearly, someone, probably at the bank, knows about the gift mortgages that are being investigated in Alaska and is playing copycat. Right now, what Rutherford Bank and Trust is doing is not illegal, as in you can go to jail. But it is questionable enough that all the mortgages might be declared null, and all the moneys therein will have to be returned. Will that happen? Probably. Will it happen soon? Maybe. Most likely there will be a decision by the SEC muckety-mucks fairly quickly. That's why we are tagging all the Mortgage Reconveyance documents. When the boom comes down, we want to catch all the rats in the same trap at the same time.

"AWS, As We Speak, five individuals and a bank have been recycling money to pick up property. There has not been a net dollar loss yet. In fact, no actual money as in paper dollars have been used. Basically, the five are getting gift mortgages and then using the money to buy raw land and foreclosed property from the same bank. The bank must love it because it is using federal mortgage money, not its own, and writing off the gift mortgage as a loss—which, unfortunately, at this moment, is legal. Then the mortgage money comes back to the bank as income when the five individuals buy raw land or foreclosed property from the bank.

"Here is where it gets complicated. Though the bank is getting mortgage money back, it is not income. This is because the mortgage money is buying other property. The bank buys foreclosed property at bargain basement prices and sells it as a mortgage at the appraised value—

which is legal—and then gifts the property back. It is very clever. The bank gets a five hundred thousand dollars home in foreclosure for one hundred thousand dollars and then gift mortgages it to an individual for five hundred thousand dollars. The bank then writes off the five hundred thousand dollars as a bad loan, and the five hundred thousand dollars come right back out the bank's front door for the next piece of foreclosed property. The reason we have not caught it before was that everything that is being done is all legal. That's because our regulations require us to look at every step of this process as a unique transaction. We didn't string everything together.

"Now we know differently, and I expect that the regulations are going to change by the end of the year. The federal government is losing quite a bit of tax revenue with this sleight of hand. If Rutherford Bank and Trust is doing it, every other bank in Nevada—and probably America—is doing it as well.

"As to the properties, looking at the map you can see that the property being bought appears to be random. Over this one area of six city blocks, there are one hundred twenty-seven lots of varying sizes. A year ago, there were sixty homes in foreclosure, twenty-nine about to go into foreclosure, and fifteen pieces of raw land. Within this acreage are twenty-three pieces of property that are in good stead. They range from a one-hundred-twenty-unit condo association to a dozen single-family homes. Today, the gift mortgaging has put all the raw land and homes that have actually gone into foreclosure into a single shell company, Juggernaut of Los Angeles, which has one owner: Jeremy Mooney, who is also the mortgage vice-president at Rutherford Bank and Trust. So far, he has kept his nose clean. As long as he *personally* does not have anything to do with the gift mortgages, he's in the clear, and what is happening is legal.

"We are not sure what Juggernaut is going to do with the land. All we know for certain is what it is *not going* to do. It is not going to be a casino or hotel. It's too far from the Strip to be a casino even if there is enough land for a casino. Same goes for a hotel. It could be a land development operation, but that land has a real value of close to ninety million dollars, and a sale that large will take some time to consummate. That's the one advantage we have with Juggernaut. We can take our time because it cannot sell that land overnight. Next year, when the gift mortgaging is determined to be in violation of the law, we'll swoop down and rearrange their plans.

"Now the bad news: these other six properties. What appears to have happened is that Jerome Foltz, once again, has managed to slime his way into a scheme. The Juggernaut properties seem to be relatively straightforward. Juggernaut is absorbing properties to end up with a large chunk of land away from the Strip, which will probably be held so it can be sold to a home developer. Looking at the legal records, it appears that Juggernaut formed a subsidiary company, Acme—and I am not making this up—where Jerome Foltz is the sole owner. Some of the properties in the gift-mortgage process are passing through Juggernaut into Acme. It is these properties, the ones ending up in Acme that are near the Strip, that have been raising eyebrows and the reason we are here.

"This is where the problem is and the reason you are all here today. Foltz, who is the sole owner of Acme, now has six different pieces of property in six different blocks that are individually almost exclusively owned by three casinos and three hotels. These six properties are giving the Nevada Gaming Control Board heartburn. There is nothing illegal about owning shares in multiple casinos and hotels that are competitors, but it is quite another to be a large shareholder in those same casinos and hotels. There are some antitrust issues that have to be worked out, but that is not the big problem. The elephant in the room right now is that Foltz and Cypress Casino appear to have been flirting with money sources on the East Coast, which concerns both the Nevada Gaming Control Board and the FBI. There is nothing solid—yet—but we, the FBI and the SEC, want a very close look at every document and agreement between and among the casinos, hotels, and Foltz. We find it hard to believe that these agreements are at an arm's length. The reason we can demand to see the documents is that the original money that bought the property was a gift mortgage, and the original mortgage was made with federal money. That gives a right to peek at the documents. That's why we're here."

CHAPTER 33

LAS VEGAS SCANDAL,
INC. RETURNS

Wednesday morning, ten seconds before high noon, Walter Otterburg, publisher/editor/reporter for *Las Vegas Scandal, Inc.* got the call of his career. It combined SLEAZE, corruption, organized crime, fraud, and dirty laundry. The only thing it was missing was sex, but that, Otterburg was sure, was going to come out of the wash.

The phone call had been from an anonymous source, which, in Otterburg's world, was nothing exceptional. Almost all of his tips came in from anonymous sources. He'd listen to anyone. But he eliminated almost everyone who called with the question, "Do you have any proof?"

In this case the anonymous caller did. Was Otterburg aware of the fact that Jerome Foltz was quietly fronting for East Coast money to establish not *one* but as many as six hotels and casinos in Las Vegas with a relative of Tony the Ant? Otterburg was interested because in Las Vegas, the term "East Coast Money" was synonymous with "mob money." Further, in Las Vegas, the best-known mobster who was gone and not lamented was Anthony "Tony the Ant" Spilotro, and even his name sent shivers down the backs of the old-timers.

177

"Right," said Otterburg. "Yuh got any proof?"

"Yeah," said the caller. "Foltz was a one hundred percent owner of a shell company named Acme, out of Los Angeles, which had picked up—*for free!*—six pieces of property in six different blocks in downtown Las Vegas within two blocks from the Strip that were individually almost exclusively owned by three casinos and three hotels. Copies of the incorporation documents for Acme and titles for the six pieces of property were, as a matter of fact, in an envelope next to his front door. A similar package had just been delivered to the chair of the Nevada Gaming Control Board."

The caller hung up before Otterburg could ask a single question about Anthony "Tony the Ant" Spilotro's connection to Jerome Foltz.

CHAPTER 34

THE NEVADA GAMING CONTROL BOARD GETS AN ENVELOPE

Wednesday afternoon, a few seconds after the offices of the Nevada Gaming Control Board emptied out for lunch, a Manilla envelope was delivered to the temporary secretary at the front desk. It was dropped on the counter while she was scrounging the refrigerator for her sack lunch. The name of the chair of the commission was on the envelope, so she just put it in the chair's mail slot.

At 1:30 that afternoon, an anonymous caller asked the chair's administrative assistant if the chair had received the envelope yet. When the administrative assistant said he was not sure, the caller said that the chair had better take a look at the documents therein because Walter Otterburg was going to be calling.

Soon.

CHAPTER 35

THE STATE OF NEVADA BANK AUDITORS STAND DOWN

Harry sat down, and a gnome of a man with glasses thick enough to start fire with the light of the sun stood up.

"I'm Sam Blythe with the state of Nevada bank audit division. I'd like to start with an audit joke, but there aren't any. They're all true stories. I'm the odd man out here because all we do is audit bank transactions. Even after hearing everything that's been said here, frankly, from the point of view of an auditor, there is nothing illegal happening. Suspicious, yes. Underhanded, yes. Sleazy, yes. But until we in the field receive specific instructions from someone up there," he pointed upward, ". . . and I do not mean *the* God, I mean *the gods* in Carson City, all I and my staff can do is what we have always done: look over the books at Rutherford Bank and Trust. That being said, we, the auditors, have been instructed by the gods in Carson City to support your efforts. What that means in nuts-and-bolts terms is that we will not be auditing Rutherford Bank and Trust until we get a firm ruling from the SEC as to what is legal and what is not. We do not want documents at the bank to disappear. So we are standing down. There are other banks we can audit, but, for the

180

moment, we are leaving Rutherford Bank and Trust alone. Our cover story is that we have been asked by the IRS to assist in the search for the fifty million dollars from the codicil. But, in reality, we are waiting for the SEC to make a decision. Then we will hit Rutherford Bank and Trust with an audit staff on steroids. The only thing we are going to do is request—and that is all we can do—that the state of California freeze the transfer of any of the properties out of Acme. We have said nothing about the SEC, and the state of California has not asked. Again and again, until the SEC makes a firm ruling on these gift mortgages, our hands are tied. Until the SEC makes that ruling, mum's the word."

CHAPTER 36

DOBBINS FREED

"Harold Dobbins—Room 1356" had started as a joke in the Room Service Department of the Excelsior Hotel until the newspapers picked it up.

Then everyone was using the expression.

When someone wanted something expensive for free, the response was simply "Harold Dobbins—Room 1356." It went viral when a news anchor asked his on-screen partner if she and her new husband were going to Hawaii for their honeymoon. Her response was "Why not? Harold Dobbins—Room 1356." The comment made the newspapers, then the social media and then the term was picked by the cable channels. There were no tweets because Dobbins only had a flip-top phone and thought a hashtag was the note on his breakfast plate thanking him for choosing the Excelsior.

Dobbins was living it up. Everyone in Las Vegas who could read knew exactly why Dobbins was in the Excelsior and figured he could order anything he wanted. Sure, the taxpayers of the United States were paying for it, but, hey, he was sticking it to the IRS! Not that many people could do that—and with the backing of a federal judge, no less!

Dobbins loved it! He couldn't afford steak on his pension, but in the Excelsior, it was "Harold Dobbins—Room 1356." He could not stand Scotch, but when it came to champagne, "Harold Dobbins—Room 1356." The porn channel didn't interest him, but the movie channels did, and it was "Harold Dobbins—Room 1356." In-between the movie, he entertained the press, talked of his days as an accountant at Cypress Casino and the sleazy place it had become, and had the reporters stay for lunch: "Harold Dobbins—Room 1356."

All good things must necessarily come to an end, and Thursday afternoon, a day ahead of the Friday deadline, Dobbins was back in federal court. The last time he had gone to court, it had been in a gray Las Vegas Police Department jumpsuit with lettering stenciled on the chest. This time he went in a sweat suit with the image of an alligator printed on the front. The gator was wearing sunglasses, a T-shirt stretched across its midriff, and it held a cocktail glass with a little umbrella in one paw. Beneath the curling tail were the words "Life ain' bad out here on the farm!"

He and the judge were tight, you know. She had let him go home to get some clothes. Escorted, of course, with the press following in his footsteps. Now he wanted to look good for the cameras—and he didn't own a tie.

The courtroom had been packed 30 seconds after the bailiff opened the doors at 2:00 p.m. for the 2:30 p.m. hearing. There were a dozen television cameras beyond the trellis, and the Defense Table was groaning under the weight of microphones. When Dobbins made it into the courtroom through a back door, he was pleasantly shocked to see so many people in the gallery. He had never been a star. Today he was. Too bad this wasn't going to last much longer.

Dobbins sat down only to rise up when it was announced that the judge was on her way in.

"All rise!"

The moment the judge sat down, she slammed her gavel and stared with venom out at the pulsating crowd in the gallery.

"I expect absolute silence in this courtroom during proceedings. If there is any show of emotion, I will clear the courtroom of people, cameras, and microphones. This is not a circus."

There was some mumbling and then the judge said, "I believe I have made myself clear." Then the court went silent.

"Mr. Dobbins, I see that you are here. From what I hear on the news, you have been treated, shall we say, very well."

"Yes, your honor."

"Hopefully this matter will be resolved quickly, and you can go back to your regular life."

"Yes, your honor."

Then she looked up. "For this hearing I want representatives of the IRS and the United States Attorney's Office to be present. I want this matter terminated today. I do not want any lingering legal issues. Will a representative from each of these agencies please sit at the Prosecutor's Table?"

There was a bit of a hubbub before two individuals burst out of the crowd in the galley and opened the gate in the trellis. One was Jane Titterington. Dobbins did not recognize the attorney, but he was a cookie-cutter image of the other older white-haired men who had been in state court on Monday.

"Your names for the record," it was stated in flat, professional voice.

The two identified themselves and sat down.

"Specifically to you, Ms. Titterington," the judge said, eyeballing the IRS agent, "you have been charged with retrieving the codicil and authenticating it. Has that been done?"

"Yes, you honor."

"And?"

"It is complicated, your honor."

"No, it is not *complicated*." The judge accented the word "complicated." "Did you open the safety deposit box of Jean Peters?"

"Yes, but . . ."

"But what?"

"We found the codicil, and the front matched the photocopy we received from a reliable source."

"And?"

"On the back of the codicil we found a note to Jean Peters from a William Whitford written on the document. It read, 'This will make you a very rich woman.'"

"Who is William Whitford?"

"We don't know."

"Did you try to find him?"

"Yes, your honor, but there are a lot of William Whitfords in the world. Further, we have no date on the back of the codicil, so we cannot determine when it was written."

"Was there ever a William Whitford who worked for Howard Hughes?"

"We could not find one, your honor."

"Was there a date on the front of the codicil?"

"Yes, January 1971. That would have been about the time that Howard Hughes was getting divorced from Jean Peters."

"The other Jean Peters?"

"Yes, your honor."

"Does the signature on the codicil match Howard Hughes's signature?"

"Yes, your honor, but anyone can find Howard Hughes's signature on the Internet. Someone with a steady hand could have copied it."

"*Could* have. That does not sound definitive to me."

Before Titterington could respond, the representative of the United States Attorney for Nevada stepped.

"We still find the possibility compelling, your honor."

"*I* don't, and I'm the one in the black robe here. Has the IRS found any evidence that Mr. Dobbins—and specifically Mr. Dobbins in his own name—had fifty million dollars, has spent fifty million dollars or bought anything that is worth fifty million dollars?"

"No, your honor. Other than his pension, Social Security, and his home, he has no other investments."

"None? No business partnerships, shell corporations?"

"None of record in any state, your honor."

"That would lead a normal person to assume that he never had the fifty million dollars."

"Well, there is still Jean Peters. She has investments."

"Can you trace those investments to a free-flying fifty million dollars?"

"No, your honor, but—"

The judge cut her off.

"Let me make sure that I understand what we have here. Mr. Dobbins is being held as a material witness while you authenticate a codicil allegedly written by a man who has been dead for half a century to a woman who has been dead for two decades, which gives fifty million dollars you cannot find to a woman who has no link to Howard Hughes. The codicil was given to the woman who has no connection to Howard Hughes by a man you cannot locate, who wrote a note on the back of the codicil with no date. You cannot find a scrap of evidence that Mr. Dobbins ever received, spent, laundered, or set up a shell company to hide the money."

"Well," replied the attorney, "we don't look at it quite that way."

"I do. Case dismissed. With prejudice. Do not bring this matter back to my attention unless you have absolute, solid proof that shows an ink-and-paper, rock-solid link between Mr. Dobbins and fifty million dollars."

The gavel came down, and that was that.

CHAPTER 37

THE CAT'S PAW

Jigger put the mouse arrow on the white X in the red square at the top of his computer screen, and the URL imploded. "That finishes that," he said as he spun around to face the others. "All the money from the sale has bounced through four banks here in the Bahamas. You've all got ten million dollars each in your individual accounts."

"They got one hell of a deal," said Bullet. "Havill & Elliot got one hundred million dollars' worth of property for fifty million dollars—ten million dollars less than their low-ball offer—with nothing to stop them from building right away. Deals like that don't come down the pike every day. They have settled fast just like we thought they would."

Frankincense chuckled. "Well, we sure got the brass ring this time."

Jigger slowly picked up his Clausthaler. "My only regret is that I can't celebrate with Scotch. I'm too old to change my ways." Then he said to Zapata, Dolores, and Myrrh, "As Shakespeare said, 'All's well that ends well.'"

"I have to be honest with you, Jigger," said Zapata. "I didn't think this was going to work. I figured the plan would fall apart before we got the big bucks, but here's to you." She raised her bloody mary as a toast.

187

"We all played it right," said Bullet over the lip of the margarita as he nudged the umbrella aside with his nose. He'd have to get used to those little umbrellas because he was never going to make himself another drink again. Now he could afford to be served.

Jigger stood up and walked to the railing of the penthouse. He looked down at the swimming pool in the center of the condo high rise and then off toward the Caribbean. Other than the occasional hurricane, life here in the Bahamas was going to be enjoyable, something he had never experienced before. Then he turned around. "We made our money before the SEC changed the rules. We're in the clear as long as we pay our usual income taxes. Then we just sit here for a year or two and wait for the heat to die down. I don't think it's a good idea for any of us to move our money back to the States, though."

"Here's to Harold, our cat's paw," Dolores said as she raised him Mimosa. "Without him, none of this would have been possible."

Everyone raised their glass.

"Well, he's got a job," added Zapata. "I'm sure he'll find the title business a *lot more* exciting than I did. He's got it all now. And the headaches."

Everyone laughed.

"Even better," she added. "After the medical tourism to the Philippines, it appears that I'm cancer-free."

Everyone cheered.

"By the way," Bullet asked, "not that it makes any difference, who's William Whitford?"

"Was," snapped Zapata. "He was the TWA pilot who got me pregnant. He thought he was being funny by coming up with the fake codicil. I kept it around as a joke and then forgot about it. We were sure lucky when I remembered it."

"We were all lucky," said Jigger. "Ours was a once-in-a-lifetime shot at fortune. We threw the dice, and God, in his infinite wisdom—"

"Her," snapped Myrrh.

CHAPTER 38

WHAT GOES AROUND COMES AROUND

It took a month for the dust from the Hughes codicil to settle. It took another month for the press to figure out how it had been used. Not that this was the first time that had happened. But it was certainly the first time it had been used so cleverly. Otterburg did not have a problem with being used; it was his stock in trade, so when it came his time to be taken for a ride, he lived with it. Then he pieced together the entire story, something only a tabloid could legally do. Then the press quoted the *Las Vegas Scandal, Inc.* That way everyone was legally covered. The five conspirators were in the wind, so they never had the chance to rebut anything published in the *Las Vegas Scandal, Inc.* That was probably OK with them because they left Las Vegas with the greatest payout in Las Vegas history: 50 million tax-free dollars.

The pieces finally fell into place when Havill & Elliott, a small residential construction company out of Minneapolis, announced the pending construction of an ultra-high end gated community of six city blocks. The community offered a serpentine greenbelt around and about the homes, a large community swimming pool, and quiet because it was

189

well back from the Strip and had "nothing but nature" on two sides. The "nothing but nature" was courtesy of a Nevada game preserve for desert tortoises. It did not take long for tongues to wag that Havill & Elliott had picked up the six blocks for $50 million, $10 million lower than the $60 million low-ball it had been baiting Las Vegas Realtors with for years. With a discount like that, the sale went through Peters Title Company like corn through a goose. The sale had been for cash, which was unusual for a sale that large, and the money paid to Bahaman bank. Hours after the cash was transferred to another Bahaman account, the four co-conspirators in Las Vegas scattered to the wind. Jean Peters never came back from Manilla, and when Harold Dobbins went to work the day after the properties changed hands, he found a Quick Claim receipt selling him Peters Title Company for $1. When asked for a comment by the press, Dobbins held up the bill of sale, smiled, and said, "Harold Dobbins—Room 1356!"

Prof was particularly pleased with the results. He had not lost a dime in the scam, and his students had a first-hand look at Las Vegas history leaching into the Las Vegas present. Not one of his students had even come close to figuring out what was really happening. That had been their homework for the semester. They had all failed miserably, but Prof hoped it would teach them to think outside of the box. After all, here was a real world, in your face, lesson in how someone else can think outside of the box and walk away with bucks that even the Strip calls "big."

In his wrap-up at the end of the semester, Prof started with a bit of history (of course!) and noted that the rise of John Calvin was the origin of the concept that money was proof of God's grace. If you made money, you were good in the eyes of God. In that case, the five conspirators were pretty damn well blessed in God's eyes.

The real-world lesson of the Hughes codicil, he told his class, was that the five conspirators were successful because they had combined surprise and speed. To be successful, they were required to move fast. They had. The scam could only be done with a small group of people who absolutely trusted each other. Prof did not bring up the fact that the five were long-term sexual trading partners, and this was most likely the glue that held them together. That made them the equivalent of a family. It would not have been possible for five people who did not trust each other to the bottom of their hearts to stay organized long enough to pull off the greatest scam in Las Vegas history—and a legal one at that. Perhaps that was saying something about sex being a stronger bind than money. Prof could not say and did not ask his class to speculate.

The key to their success, he told his class, was more than planning. It was transforming those plans into action. Many businesses plan and plan and plan but never take the next step. Plans are like a powerful race car in idle; unless you shift into gear, the car just sits there. The conspirators leaped into action. They got something done while others were still talking about it. They were now $50 million richer, while the same other people were talking about what had happened. Five percent of all people make things happen. Ten percent of people watch things happen, and eighty-five percent of all people want to know what happened.

Just as important, and he finished the semester with this warning, the success of the Hughes codicil episode was *not* one based on "catching a seam." Prof used the football example, as it was the most appropriate for his real-world lesson. "Catching a seam," Prof noted, was a football term that implied finding a weakness in the defense. Looking for, finding, and taking advantage of a weakness is the sign of a good team in football. You play your strength against your opponent's weakness. This is not, he emphasized, what happened with the five co-conspirators. They did not find a so-called weakness in the banking and real-estate businesses either singly or doubly. They came up with a totally new card game. And it was a card game, he emphasized, because it was done legally and developed permutations no one had seen before. They may not have been the first to pull off this kind of a scam, just the first of such a scam to hit the big-time in terms of both money and publicity. They did not "catch a seam," in the sense that they played by the established rules of the game. They came up with a new approach that will—and very quickly, he added—generate regulations and statutes to make sure that no one else does what these men and women had done. For the five

191

conspirators in the wind, it will be closing the barn door after the horse has been stolen. They will go into the text books as a legal scam that worked but one that will not be legal ever again.

Six months after the five conspirators disappeared, the last shoe dropped. In a rare, joint press conference, the IRS, SEC, and the Nevada Gaming Control Board announced the wrap-up of the matter of Jerome Foltz and his land acquisition. They, collectively, determined that while there was no specific law or regulation Foltz had violated, his ownership of six lots in six different blocks put him dangerously close to having a significant conflict of interest if a casino, hotel, or casino with hotels, or a combination thereof were built on more than one lot. He was ordered to sell five lots.

However, as the collected agencies noted, the fact of the matter was that Foltz's corporation, Acme, was actually a subsidiary of Juggernaut of Los Angeles. Juggernaut of Los Angeles had been legally transferred in toto from the ownership of one Jeremy Mooney to Harold Charles Dobbins. Juggernaut had originally contained 94 properties, of which 93 had been sold to Havill & Elliot, a housing contractor in Minneapolis. This left one piece of property in Juggernaut of Los Angeles, the legal minimum for the corporation to remain solvent. Juggernaut of Los Angeles had the minimum required value of $1, the value of the lot when it was transferred to Juggernaut by the previous owner, Jean Peters.

Juggernaut of Los Angeles was thus the 100% owner of Acme. Acme was 100% owned by Foltz. The six lots owned by Foltz had been transferred into Acme for $1 each from Juggernaut. Therefore, both the gross and net assets of Acme was $6 for the six pieces of property. It was not the value of the property that concerned the collected agencies but the smell of impropriety. Foltz ordered to sell five of the properties "at cost" with the buyer of first resort, that being Juggernaut.

Harold Charles Dobbins, the 100% owner of Juggernaut of Los Angeles, had no problem writing Jerome Foltz a check for $5. When Foltz angrily accepted the $5 check, Dobbins allegedly snapped, "How do *you* like them apples?"

192

APPENDIX

TRUTH IS STRANGER THAN FICTION

The novel you have just read is fictional.

But the saga of the gift mortgage is not.

What Jigger did in *the Hughes codicil* is legal and most likely being done in every city in the United States as you are reading this sentence. It's a legal way that bank muckety-mucks can give their buddies and "deserving individuals" free money.

I discovered the practice by accident. I was investigating four murders in Anchorage, Alaska, which had occurred in the 1940s and 1950s. Even though the murders were old, there were some alleged perpetrators still alive. (I have to say alleged because none of them have gone to trial.)

Then my life went through the toilet and into the cesspool.

Fifteen year later I discovered why.

The murders had been *allegedly* paid for by Alaska's first billionaire. His son was the president of the bank that his father founded—National Bank of Alaska—which was bought out by Wells Fargo in 1999. *Someone* in Wells Fargo in Alaska clearly did not want me doing a book on the internal machinations of the bank when it came to murder. Then *that someone* used the full faith and credit of Wells Fargo in Alaska to use mortgage money—federal money—to have me fired from jobs that I did

195

have and keep me from getting jobs for which I should have reasonably been considered.

My complaints in writing with documentation were sent out the Anchorage Office of the Federal Bureau of Investigation (FBI), the Securities and Exchange Commission (SEC), the Internal Revenue Service (IRS), and the Consumer Financial Protection Bureau (CFPB). The more I looked into land records, the more gift mortgages I found. To date I have discovered about $150 million of these "free money" mortgages to mayors, police chiefs, attorney generals, at least one governor, and many private citizens. A few of the real letters I sent to the FBI, SEC, IRS, and CFPB are included in this Appendix.

If gift mortgages are being given freely in Alaska, they are being given freely in your state as well. If you want to make America a better place—and make yourself money at the same time—do what I did. Find gift mortgages in your state and report them with the documentation to the FBI office in your state, the SEC, IRS, and CFPB. If any of these agencies go after the perpetrators and collect money, you get a percentage. All this is so easy that even I did it, and I have no background in banking, finance, law, law enforcement, or the judicial system.

How do you do it?

Stated as simply as possible, pull up the land records in your state. Most states have gone electronic, so you should be able to find the records online. In Alaska they are listed under the Department of Natural Resources. In your state the land records are likely listed under the Recorder's Office under the Department of Administration or the Department of Revenue.

The site should have a name index. That's where you start. Begin by inputting the names of people you think are sleazy. What you are looking for are Mortgages of Reconveyance. These are the records of mortgage payoffs. Match the Mortgage of Reconveyance document with the original mortgage document. If your sleazy individual got a mortgage from the First National Bank of Whatever on January 1, 2015, and received a Mortgage of Reconveyance for the same property on February 15, 2015, I suggest that this person got a gift mortgage. He—

or she—probably didn't pay any taxes on that gift mortgage because paying off a debt is not income.

Once you jump in the records, you will discover just how complicated the system is. People may own land under a variety of names, just like in the novel. You may find that John T. Smith has land listed as John. T. Smith, John Smith, J. T. Smith, or J. Smith. This is John T. Smith's way of hiding his ownership. Also check with the corporation lists in your state. John T. Smith may have formed a corporation and then put the land in the name of the corporation. Corporate and business names are also public information, and you should be able to find them on your state's web page. They are probably under the Department of Commerce or, once again, Department of Administration.

You are going to have problems when you search for common names like John T. Smith. What I did was find the name of John T. Smith's wife and searched for Sarah or Jane Smith, for instance. When I found a John T. Smith with Sarah or Jane, I was pretty sure I had the right couple. But even if I could not find the right couple, if I found a John T. Smith and Jeanine Smith who had a gift mortgage, I reported them.

If there is a reward, you will have earned it. Even more important, banks have to be taught that mortgage money is federal money, public money, and not cash in their till they can give to anyone they want for any reason.

Be aggressive.

Punch up the names of mayors, police chiefs, municipal, county and state prosecutors, attorney generals, nonprofit board members, legislators, assembly member, and other public figures. I am sure that once you start this process, you will be as shocked as I was. If enough of us "little people" yell and scream, maybe, just maybe, we can force the banks to be responsible with our money.

Over the long term, support candidates of either party who advocate for more regulation of the banking industry or, better yet, break the big banks up into smaller ones. Banks that are "too big to fail" are going to cause another mortgage disaster like we had in 2008. It's only a matter of time.

If you *really* want to do something about big banks but find that the political parties in your state—or Washington, DC—do not have the backbone to solve the gift-mortgage problem, here's a suggestion. Have your state's housing office simply take the place of the banks. There is no reason for John and Mary Jones to have to go to a bank to get a housing loan. The money they are going to be getting through the chain of banks is actually their own money. It is federal money from the federal government.

There is no reason for banks to be involved in the mortgage transaction at all. Have the state of Whatever borrow the money, not the banks. There is no reason for banks to be involved at all. If your state acts as the bank, it will save your state millions of dollars. Instead of the state legislature appropriating millions of dollars for the state of Whatever Housing Authority for the wide range of mortgage support most states offer, just fund the staff of the housing authority through the loans it is making. Then borrow all—100%—loans for all residential homes up to, say, $500,000 from Fannie Mae or Freddie Mac. Better yet, add half a percentage to the money from Fannie Mae or Freddie Mac and then the state of Whatever will not have to allocate any state money for the housing authority.

An even better suggestion would be to have no federal money loaned to the banks. After all, that's tax money—our money. We, the people, pay taxes for the betterment of the people, all of us. Why should the banks get public money at all, much less at low interest loans, and pass on the *bad news* to borrowers? The banks are private businesses; let them make their own money on loans of their own money, not the public's money. Some will say that *the public* is paid back handsomely for letting the banks borrow at low interest. Really? In 2008 *alone* the U.S. government spent *$900 billion* to bail out the banks—and not a single banker went to jail, while citizens lost *$3.4 trillion* in real-estate wealth, about $30,000 in equity per house in the United States!

Worse, not a single legislative brake has been put in place to stop another real-estate meltdown. As of the publishing of this book, gift mortgages are still being given. As of the publishing of this book, the banks are still making a profit off *your* money. As of the publishing of this book, if you are buying your home honestly, then you better get a firm grip on your tutu, because there is going to be another real-estate meltdown. Congress isn't doing anything to stop the banks from speculative lending, and the federal government isn't enforcing the regulation on the books to avert another disaster. So if the federal government can't/ won't/isn't helping, or is helpless, to stop another financial disaster, it's up to the states—your state in particular. Your state has to step up to the plate and take charge of—at least—the real-estate loans in your state.

You say it can't be done?

Really?

Take some advice from Prof.

Read you history.

Specifically read the Constitution of the United States. *Banking is not a power* of the U.S. government. There is nothing on banking in the U.S. Constitution.

Read your history.

If you don't know where to start, look under Alexander Hamilton on Wikipedia and start from there. Then punch up Andrew Jackson and read about his fight with the Second Bank of the United States. Then read the Tenth Amendment to the Constitution:

The powers not delegated to the United States by the Constitution, nor prohibited by it to the States, are reserved to the States respectively, or to the people.

There is nothing in the U.S. Constitution that *precludes states from borrowing mortgage money from Fannie Mae and Freddie Mac.*

Now save your state *millions and millions* of state dollars by having your state become the mortgage lender for all residential housing in your state. Depending on your state's constitution, your governor may even have the power to do it on his or her own. There's a quick way to save millions of state dollars without raising taxes, downsizing staff, or cutting back on services. Even better for your state, John and Mary Jones will get their loan at prime. That lowers their monthly house payment substantially and puts more actual cash into your state's economy.

Even better, spread the interest payments over the life of the loan. Currently, banks front-load the interest. That's why you are paying so much on interest in the early years of your loan. The bank wants to get its share first. By spreading the interest evenly over the life of the loan, home-loan borrowers will build equity faster. That will give them more money to borrow if they need a Second Mortgage or want to move up to a better home.

If you really want to improve your state's economy immediately, start refinancing homes. Start with the ones with the highest interest rates first. This will drop house payments substantially, and a good chunk of those savings will end up being spent in the local economy.

As you read the authentic letters and the associated documentation in this Appendix, keep in mind the prescient quote from philosopher George Santayana: "Those who do not learn from the past are doomed to repeat it."

UPDATE MARCH 2018

On August 2017, I filed a Writ of Mandamus to force the federal government to look into gift mortgages. The Writ was approved, and in March 2018, it was sent to the SEC, IRS, CFPB, and the Federal Housing Finance Administration.

UNITED STATES DISTRICT COURT
AT ANCHORAGE, ALASKA

Steven C. Levi, Pro Se
 	
                   Plaintiff,
 	
vs.
 	
Federal Housing Finance Agency,
Consumer Finance Protection Bureau,
Security and Exchange Commission and
Internal Revenue Service
 	
               Defendants
	)
	)
	)
	)
	)
	)
	)
	)
	)
	)
	)
	)
		CASE NO:
		3:17-cv-000183-TMB

MOTION FOR A WRIT OF MANDAMUS

FACTS OF THE CASE

Over the past decade plaintiff has uncovered what plaintiff labels "gift mortgages." These are mortgages which a bank lists as paid in full and then either writes off the loan as a bad debt or passes the loss back to the Federal Housing Finance Corporation. Either way, the individual ends up with a free home. It is assumed by the plaintiff – see correspondence from the Internal Revenue Service, Exhibit 2 – that no income tax is paid on the free home because a mortgage is a debt and paying off a debt is not income. An example of three gift mortgages is Exhibit 1. Federal law requires mortgage moneys to be used exclusively for mortgages. Plaintiff contends signing for a mortgage which is going to be quickly forgiven is a violation of federal law.

Plaintiff has reported in excess of $100 million in suspected gift mortgages to the Federal Housing Finance Corporation, Security and

Exchange Commission and the Consumer Financial Protection Bureau. No action has been taken other by these bodies other than opening complaint files. Alaska's population is $1/400^{th}$ of that of the United States. If providing gift mortgages is an industry standard, this equates to $40 billion nationwide. To date, no agency has informed plaintiff that gift mortgages are legal. Plaintiff believes gift mortgages to be a violation of federal law.

Plaintiff's research has revealed the documentation required to trace land ownership and mortgage lending to be, at best, convoluted. The public record of Alaska's land transactions is byzantine and appears more designed to confuse than enlighten. For this additional reason, action by the United States government is required.

PETITIONER'S STANDING

Plaintiff is a resident, citizen and tax payer of the United States. The existence and continued use of gift mortgages reduces the income to the United States government and allows select individuals free use of taxpayer moneys in the form of property.

RESPONDENT'S CAPACITY

All defendants in this MOTION FOR A WRIT OF MANDAMUS have the ability and legal authority to resolve this issue.

REAL PARTY IN INTEREST'S CAPACITY

The real party in this MOTION FOR A WRIT OF MANDAMUS is the American taxpayer.

CASE MEETS PROCEDURAL REQUIREMENTS

This MOTION FOR A WRIT OF MANDAMUS is unusual in that there are no specific procedural requirements which exist for plaintiff other than filing a complaint. A complaint has been filed with the Securities and Exchange Commission (1421170532539), the Consumer Financial Protection Bureau (160218-001034), and the Federal Housing Finance Agency. The Securities and Exchange Commission and the Consumer Financial Protection Bureau have done nothing more than opening a file and including correspondence from the plaintiff. The Federal Housing Finance Agency has not responded to plaintiff's letters. The Internal Revenue Service, Exhibit 2, informed plaintiff it was rejecting his complaint because plaintiff "did not provide specific or credible information regarding tax underpayments or violations of internal revenue laws." With specific regard to the Internal Revenue Service, plaintiff can only assume recipients of gift mortgages did not pay income tax as plaintiff has no access to gift mortgage recipients' tax returns. Plaintiff disputes gift mortgages are "not violations of internal revenue laws."

WHY DECISIONS ARE INVALID

No agency which has received the complaints of gift mortgages has made a determination as to the legality of gift mortgages. Further, no agency which has received the complaints has indicated that any action has taken place or will take place.

ADMINISTRATIVE REMEDIES

Plaintiff has exhausted all administrative remedies. Other than filing complaints there are no other administrative remedies.

PRAYER FOR RELIEF

Plaintiff prays that the United States District Court at Anchorage will order the Federal Housing Finance Agency to request a complete list of all mortgages in Alaska which have been recorded as paid off under whatever terms indicate a return of the title of the property to the owner. Then the Federal House Finance Agency is ordered to compare the list from the State of Alaska, Department of Natural Resources, Recorder's Office with loans which were not paid off according to the records of the Federal Housing Finance Agency. When a match is made, the individual who benefited from the gift mortgage is ordered reported to the Internal Revenue Service for a determination of taxes owed as well as the legality of the gift mortgage process. Further, when a match is made, the Securities and Exchange Commission is ordered to investigate the legality of each specific gift mortgage and the culpability of the lending institution(s) which approved the gift mortgage. Further still, when a complete list of matches is made, the Consumer Financial Protection Bureau is ordered to determine the legality of the gift mortgage process and the culpability of the lending institution(s). Finally, if the Federal Housing Finance Agency finds in excess of $25 million of gift mortgages in Alaska alone, the Federal Housing Finance Agency is ordered to search for and prosecute gift mortgages in all other jurisdictions under its financial umbrella.

Filed this 18th day of August, 2017.

Steven C. Levi